THE S

SORCERER

Their way was littered with corpses and discarded weapons. Numerous fights continued, with the enemy still swarming aboard. Shani was in no mood for gentle persuasion. If she couldn't go around a living obstacle she carved her way through.

Tycho was the object of more than one blow. Blades, knives and clubs bounced harmlessly off his supernaturally toughened hide, leaving his attackers stupefied.

As they passed a Delgarvian trooper a grappling-hook flew over and buried itself in his back. The line it was attached to pulled taut and he smashed into the rail. Shani quickly severed the rope. But her comrade was beyond help.

"The odds are too great, Tycho," she said. "We're losing!"

Also available in the Point Fantasy series:

POINT
FANTASY

THE SHADOW OF THE

SORCERER

Stan Nicholls

■SCHOLASTIC

Scholastic Children's Books
Commonwealth House, 1–19 New Oxford Street,
London WC1A 1NU, UK
a division of Scholastic Ltd
London ~ New York ~ Toronto ~ Sydney ~ Auckland

First published by Scholastic Ltd, 1997

Copyright © Stan Nicholls, 1997

ISBN 0 590 13971 1

Typeset by TW Typesetting, Midsomer Norton, Somerset
Printed by Cox & Wyman Ltd, Reading, Berks.

10 9 8 7 6 5 4 3 2 1

*For Helen and Tony Inman, for friendship
and support Above and Beyond*

PRELUDE

What has gone before…

It was an age of legends.

A time of heroism and black villainy. An era of magic and flashing blades, of harmony and war, sorrow and hope.

And Dalveen Leandor was its greatest warrior.

His origins were shrouded in mystery. Abandoned as a baby on the steps of a temple in Allderhaven, capital of Delgarvo, he was found by Golcar Quixwood, Commander of the Imperial Guard. Delgarvo's monarch, King Eldrick, was mourning his queen, who had died only hours before. Yet he accepted the child into his household at Torpoint, the royal palace. The boy was raised with Eldrick's daughter, Princess Bethan, and from his earliest years displayed a genius for the martial

1

arts. Under Quixwood's guidance these skills were nurtured and honed.

By young adulthood, Dalveen knew no equal as a swordsman, and had been appointed King's Champion. He and Bethan were betrothed. And a fondness for black garb, along with his lethal fighting talents and brooding nature, earned him a new name among the people.

Nightshade.

Eldrick's benign rule made Delgarvo a land of peace and justice in a turbulent world. But a threat arose from an unexpected quarter. Corrupted by the dark side of sorcery, Court Magician Avoch-Dar plotted to overthrow the King. Learning of this treachery, Dalveen exposed him. Eldrick banished Avoch-Dar to the desert wastes of remote Vaynor. His leniency was misplaced. The wizard returned to seek revenge at the head of an army of human malcontents and inhuman hellspawn.

The forces of Light and Darkness clashed in a mighty battle. But before the sorcerer was driven back he used his foul magic to destroy Nightshade's sword arm. Wounded in body and pride, Dalveen retreated to barren Hawkstone mountain. There he lived in solitude for a year, teaching himself to fight left-handed.

Then Avoch-Dar attacked again, and this time conquered Delgarvo, taking the King and Bethan hostage.

Dalveen was powerless to act until sought out by Melva, an aged wise woman. She was the keeper of a millennia-old prophecy which told of Avoch-Dar's rise and the terrible fate in store for Humanity. It also spoke of a champion born to oppose him. Convinced Nightshade was the prophesied hero, Melva explained that to stand a chance against such evil, and perhaps restore his arm, he must recover the fabled Book of Shadows. An incredibly ancient compendium of magical lore, the book belonged to a race of long vanished demons.

Having passed on the prophecy, Melva died.

To achieve his task, Dalveen had to travel to the forbidding, horror haunted isle of Zenobia. Three companions joined his quest. Shani Vanya was an expert knife-thrower who had seen her family wiped out by the wizard's followers. Craigo Meath was a soldier of fortune. And Tycho was neither man nor beast. An homunculus, a being magically created by Avoch-Dar, he had escaped the wizard's cruelty. Together they overcame the deadly perils left by the demons to protect the Book of Shadows.

When Dalveen gained the tome he found it more than a mere book. A kind of malignant intelligence radiated from it. In some strange way it seemed alive.

A fraction of its awesome power transported the group back to Delgarvo, where their luck turned sour. The book failed to renew Dalveen's arm. Meath was revealed as a traitor, one of the sorcerer's lieutenants, and he lured the others into a trap. Forced to duel with the mercenary, who wielded an enchanted sword, Dalveen needed all his expertise to slay him. But Avoch-Dar recited a dreadful spell from the book, opening a gateway to the realm in which the demons now dwelt. The vile horde poured through.

In the chaos that followed, Avoch-Dar's occupation of Delgarvo was broken and his forces routed. Fleeing with the demons to their dimension, he took the Book of Shadows with him.

He left behind an enchanted crystal.

And Nightshade's despair.

CHAPTER 1

It looked like they were going to hang a dozen dwarfs.

The wooden gibbets resembled small versions of gallows. There were two parallel lines of six, with a round sac made of thin animal skin suspended from each. The pouches hanging on the first gibbets were the size of ripe pumpkins. Those that followed grew progressively smaller, so that the last pair were no bigger than an infant's clenched fist.

A man walking between the gibbets with his arms outstretched and a sword in both hands might just touch the dangling sacs on either side with his blade tips.

Golcar Quixwood wondered if even Nightshade would find impossible the task he had taken on.

Dalveen Leandor sat bareback on a grey colt at the far end of the courtyard. The horse had no reins or stirrups. Leandor wore a sheathed sword, and his empty right sleeve was pinned to the side of his shirt. Light snow dusted his hair and black attire.

Men of the Palace Guard had gathered to watch. They stood in small groups, talking quietly and stamping their feet against the cold. A young cadet with a drum slung from his shoulder awaited the signal.

Quixwood turned to the mounted warrior and called, "Ready?"

Leandor nodded.

A downward stroke of Quixwood's hand set drummer and rider in motion.

The drum's tempo matched the beating of a human heart. At the first strike Leandor spurred his horse. A steaming snort hissed from the beast's nostrils as it raced off at speed across the icy cobblestones. Controlling the steed only by the pressure of his thighs, Leandor pulled free his sword.

He reached the first pair of gibbets at the drum's third beat.

His blade flashed out and slashed the hanging pouch on his left. It released a red shower of watery dye. With lightning swiftness he swung the blade to his right, leaning from the horse to gain the target. His blow was rewarded with another explosion of crimson liquid.

The drummer kept up his steady rhythm.

Leandor rode on between the rows of gibbets. Almost too rapidly for the eye to see, his sword sliced to the left, to the right and back again.

Each succeeding pair of sacs, smaller than the ones before, contained different coloured dyes. The touch of his weapon's keen steel brought wet flowerings of yellow, green, orange, blue. And as he cleaved through the last and tiniest of his marks, fine, twin puffs of glistening gold.

The drumming ceased. Applause and cheers rang out from the spectators.

Leandor's horse thundered on. He squeezed its flanks with his knees, slowing the charge a little. Then in one flowing movement he turned, lifting his leg over the animal's back, and from side-saddle position slid off. He landed deftly on his feet and re-sheathed the sword. Further on, the horse was stopped and calmed by a groom.

The onlookers began drifting back to their duties, some chattering and laughing. Coins changed hands in settlement of wagers. An attendant ran over and draped Leandor with a cloak. The snowfall was heavier.

As the servant hurried away, Quixwood arrived. He slapped Leandor's back. "Magnificent!" he boomed. "Thirteen beats. *Thirteen!* And not a spot of dye on you."

Despite the feat he had just performed, Leandor was obviously in a despondent mood. He favoured his adoptive father with a meagre, fleeting smile, but did not speak.

The two men were different in many ways.

Quixwood was approaching old age, though fit for his years. He was stoutly built, with a barrel chest and sturdy limbs. His full beard was greying, his eyes blue. Expansive by nature, his view of life was uncomplicated, and he was wont to express his opinions bluntly.

Leandor was young. Wiry and athletic, he was at the peak of his agility. His face was clean-shaven, his eyes of olive tint. Gathered into a ponytail, his long black hair hung half-way down his back. The dark-hued clothes he favoured reflected his character, for he was inclined to melancholy.

They were alike in choosing to live by the sword.

Quixwood glanced at Torpoint's massive frontage. Craftsmen swarmed on scaffolding erected against the palace's great wall. Springy boards supported by uprights of lashed oak trunks bore masons labouring to repair breached stonework. Buckets of mortar were winched up through swirling snow.

"The work progresses well," he said.

"Not well enough," Leandor replied grimly.

"You're pushing yourself too hard, Dalveen. It's been five months since Avoch-Dar's invasion and you've hardly rested since."

"We have to put right the destruction he caused and rebuild our defences. With winter closing in, time is short."

"Aye, but you could at least delegate some of your responsibilities."

"I need to keep my mind occupied." He indicated his vacant sleeve with a jab of his thumb. "It prevents me thinking about this."

"The loss of a fighter's sword arm isn't something you quickly come to terms with, lad. Maybe you never do. And having that damn book snatched away, along with any chance it held of restoring your limb ... well, you're bound to feel crushed. But you *have* to put all that behind you now."

"How can I put the sorcerer behind me? He came close to bringing us to our knees. If he returns to Delgarvo—"

"Returns? For the gods' sake, man, *forget* Avoch-Dar. Even if he lives, he dwells with the demons in whatever infernal realm they occupy."

"Does he? I wonder..."

"You spend too much time wondering, and brooding in front of that dead crystal of his."

"He has the book, Golcar."

"It's possible he'll make no more progress using it than you did."

"You overlook his alliance with the demons. And they created the tome."

"Maybe the wizard's still a threat and maybe he isn't. If he turns up again we'll be ready."

"I should be *doing* something. I should be out there searching for him or—"

"Or what? And searching where? Talk sense, Dalveen. You said yourself how much there is to do here in Allderhaven. We need you. Bethan needs you. She has enough to worry about with the King."

"How is he?"

Quixwood's expression grew sombre. "Not good. The physicians have been attending him again for most of the day."

"I really thought he was going to recover from that wound Avoch-Dar's minion inflicted. He seemed to be mending. But he would insist on driving himself so hard. At his age, he should have taken it easier while the injury healed."

"Just as well ask the sun not to rise. Eldrick's always been a man of action. Merely getting older didn't change that."

"True. I'll visit his chambers as soon as I've attended to one or two matters. Let's hope there's been some improvement." He fastened the clasp on his cloak. "I can't linger here, Golcar, there's too much to be done."

"All right, but practise what you preach, Dalveen, and don't drive *yourself* too hard. Remember what I said. Try to spread your workload. And leave the sorcerer and the book where they belong, in the past."

"I wish I could. But suppose they aren't in the past. What then?"

Without waiting for an answer Leandor swept towards the palace, his cloak flapping in the prickly wind.

More snow was falling from a darkening sky. It was beginning to cover the splashes of vivid colour released by Nightshade's blade.

Quixwood watched him go, and pondered his words.

If Avoch-Dar and the Book of Shadows are part of our present, he thought, *then the future's too terrible to contemplate.*

CHAPTER 2

Leandor's patience was running out.

The latest so-called healer seemed no more competent than his predecessors. Twig thin and middle-aged, with white shoulder-length hair, he went by the name Thesmesus. He arrived with Leandor's astrological chart. Then he spent half an hour explaining it was probably useless because no one knew his true time or place of birth.

Next he produced a well-thumbed grimoire, some candles, incense and a jumble of other magical paraphernalia. Selecting a spell he said was guaranteed to restore Leandor's arm, he blundered through the ritual and fluffed the lines. When he eventually got it right, nothing happened.

Now he was cooking up an evil-smelling potion in a small black cauldron.

Scooping a goblet of the seething liquid, he handed it over and announced, "This infusion should renew your arm instantly, sir."

"Instantly?"

"Providing the gods will it, of course."

"Of course," Leandor replied cynically. He eyed the concoction with suspicion. It looked like hot mud.

"You will find it most beneficial if taken in one draft," Thesmesus advised him.

Leandor raised the goblet to his lips. Trying to ignore the overpowering pungency of its content, he downed the mixture in a single gulp.

His face soured. "It tastes … *vile*. What's in it? No, on second thought I'd rather you didn't tell me."

"Nothing to cause you concern, I assure you. Now be at ease and we should shortly see the effect."

Several minutes passed in awkward silence.

Finally Leandor said, "It seems the gods aren't very co-operative today." He made no effort to hide his mockery.

Thesmesus reddened. "I don't understand it. You feel nothing? No tingling of your limb's stump? A feeling of warmth, perhaps?"

"Only a foulness in my mouth." His tone

13

softened. "You need not be embarrassed, my friend. The magic Avoch-Dar used to maim me was powerful beyond reckoning. It will not easily be undone."

The colour drained from the other man's cheeks at mention of the sorcerer.

"I thank you for your efforts," Leandor added, "but now I must attend to my duties and—" There was a knock at the chamber door. "Come!"

Thesmesus' jaw dropped when he saw the creature that entered.

It was undersized compared to a human, muscular and entirely covered in red tinged, fuzzy brown fur. A disproportionately large head topped its squat neck. The hair on its face was shorter and almost golden. Its mouth was like a man's, but its nose consisted of two flat slits, and its ears were pointed and swept back. Most striking of all were the immense spherical eyes. They were deep green and had no lids.

Wearing only wrist bands, anklets and a strip about its waist, all fashioned from metals of different colours, it clutched a parchment scroll in one of its clawed hands.

When it spoke, Thesmesus gave a little start.

"I'm sorry, Dalveen," the creature said, "am I disturbing you?"

"Not at all, Tycho. My visitor was just leaving."

They looked at the healer, who snapped out of

his reverie and mumbled, "Er … yes. Leaving. Right away." He hurriedly began gathering the implements of his trade.

Arms full of equipment, cauldron swinging from his wrist, he made an ungainly attempt at a bow while muttering apologies and farewells. Taking one last gape at Tycho, he headed for the door.

After it slammed, Leandor quietly laughed.

"It seems my appearance still has an unsettling effect on some humans," Tycho commented.

"Not many have had the pleasure of meeting an homunculus. You can't blame him."

"I don't. Was he of any help?"

"No, he's just another low grade wizard, I'm afraid. And I'm wearying of being the target for every quack and charlatan in Delgarvo. I've been prodded, pinched, chanted over, splashed with holy waters, choked by incense and given disgusting things to drink. More spells have been directed my way than you could shake a sword at." He sighed. "I know it's hopeless, but I'm doing it to please Bethan. Only the book offers a chance of returning my arm."

"I fear that is so, Dalveen."

"Is there any word from our agents concerning Avoch-Dar?"

"None. We have spies in most parts of the realm, and not one reports so much as a whisper concerning the sorcerer. Which doesn't mean he isn't plotting in secret somewhere, of course. Assuming he's still alive."

"You doubt that?"

"I would say Avoch-Dar is a very hard man to kill."

"So would I. And I'm glad you agree. Sometimes it feels as though I'm the only one who believes we haven't heard the last of him."

"During the time I spent at his court after he created me, the one lesson I learnt was that as long as he lived he would be a menace."

Leandor fell into dismal contemplation, then roused himself and said, "Forgive me, Tycho. Why are you here?"

"You'll recall that after His Majesty appointed me Chancellor of the Royal Treasury you asked me to assess the nation's finances." He placed the scroll on the table. "These are my findings."

"I'll look at them later. Talk me through the main points for now."

"That's easily done. I've had an inventory taken of the destruction wrought by Avoch-Dar's invasion, and the damage is even more extensive than we thought. Apart from the ravaged buildings here in Allderhaven, the countryside is littered with ruined bridges, aqueducts, mills, farmhouses ... it's a long list. Add to that the cost of importing wheat because of the lost harvest, plus the rebuilding work you've embarked upon, and it's a

16

grim picture. Delgarvo is near bankruptcy."

"Things are that bad?"

"I'm afraid so. If no new source of revenue is found, in a matter of a month or two there won't be enough money to pay for essentials like the army, let alone rebuilding."

"So what can we do?"

"Levy new taxes?"

"The King would never allow it, assuming he was well enough to decide the matter. And I'd not favour such a solution myself. The people have suffered enough and barely have the means to support themselves as it is."

"What, then? Because if Avoch-Dar threatened us again, or anyone else challenged Delgarvo, we could hardly afford to defend ourselves."

"I know."

"There are some valuable relics here in the palace, perhaps we could sell them off," the homunculus suggested.

"I don't think so. Finding buyers in an impoverished land would be no easy task. More importantly, it wouldn't be popular. Parting with Torpoint's heirlooms could erode people's confidence in our ability to rule properly." His sombre expression returned. "We'll have to find another way."

After his depressing conversation with Tycho,

Leandor felt he needed to take some air.

He left the palace and wandered more or less aimlessly until he came to Allderhaven's merchant quarter. For a while he almost managed to forget his worries as he mingled with the crowd in the area's colourful street markets.

An hour passed before he remembered that he had to get back for another meeting. This time he and Tycho were going to view the rebuilding work taking place on Torpoint's defences, and try to figure out a way of paying for it.

As he made for a thoroughfare that would take him home, he noticed a stranger elbowing towards him through the mass of people. Instinctively, Leandor's hand found the hilt of his sword.

The approaching man was taller than average, towering at least a head higher than those around him. He seemed beyond middle age, but looked impressively fit and of powerful physique. His back was ramrod straight. He sported a full, greying beard, and was dressed in a loose flowing brown poncho, black breeches and leather boots. The expression on his face was best described as determined.

"Dalveen Leandor?" It was as much a statement as a question.

Leandor slowly nodded and warily tightened his hold on the sword.

"I would speak with you." Again there was as

much demand as request in the man's tone.

"What is your concern?"

The stranger eyed Leandor's vacant sleeve. "One you share."

"I do not consult with would-be healers in the street. Add your name to the list of the others wanting to see me."

The man was offended. "*I* am no sawbones or charlatan sorcerer. The matter I wish to discuss is far more important."

Leandor sighed, expecting to be asked to intervene in some dispute about an inheritance, or to have to listen to a rambling complaint concerning the sewage system. "I'm in a hurry, so perhaps you could make this brief. What do you want to talk about?"

"The Book of Shadows."

"The book?" Leandor's interest was aroused, but his former suspicion also returned. "What of it?"

The stranger indicated the milling throng jostling past them. "Can we not have a little privacy?"

"Over here." Dalveen made for a slightly less busy stretch of road by a ruined wall.

"This is hardly private," the stranger complained.

"Take it or leave it. My time is limited. Now who are you, and what do you have to say about the book?"

"My name is Drew Hadzor."

It meant nothing to Leandor.

"I have two things to say about the Book of Shadows," Hadzor continued. "First, I believe you have misjudged its capacity for good."

"*Good?* That damnable tome must be the most evil thing in creation! It was the product of a wicked race, what else could it be?"

"My hypothesis is that the book's *essential* power is neither bad nor good, but that it takes on the attributes of the race or individual able to use it."

Faint alarm bells began ringing in the recesses of Leandor's mind. "A statement like that is all the better for evidence."

"I do not possess proof, exactly."

"I see."

"But my reasoning is sound. Though it would take some time to explain it."

"You said you had two points."

"Yes. The second is to do with your relationship to the book."

Dalveen raised his eyebrows, wondering what was to follow.

Hadzor slipped a hand into his poncho, brought out a flat hip flask and offered it. "Brandy?"

"No."

Gulping a deep draft, Hadzor smacked his lips appreciatively. "Perfect stuff for keeping out the cold."

Annoyed at the delay, Leandor tried bringing

him back to the point. "What *about* my relationship to the book?"

"You are a mighty warrior, Nightshade, none can deny that. I stand second to none in my admiration and respect for your martial prowess."

Dalveen suspected it was more likely this man stood second to none in admiring himself.

"And I can see how the prophecy attached to the book might be open to certain incorrect interpretations," Hadzor went on.

"Incorrect interpretations?" The alarm bells in Leandor's head were getting louder. "Have you by some chance come across one of the prophecy's missing fragments?"

"No. I base my view on such legends as exist concerning the prophecy and your own account of it, which as you know has been widely circulated by storysmiths and balladeers. I take it these versions are essentially accurate?"

"Yes. And you have reached some kind of conclusion based on them?"

"My *own* interpretation, as I implied. But I think it more convincing than yours. I mean you no offence in saying this, you understand."

"Naturally. Go on."

"When the prophecy tells of the coming of a great champion to battle the forces of evil, it could be seen as relating to you. But have you considered that there may be another who better

21

fits that role, and hence has a claim to the book?"

"No, I haven't. Because I did not set out to prove I was part of the prophecy, as you seem to think. In fact, I had never heard of it. It was a case of having to accept my destiny once the truth could no longer be denied. I neither sought nor do I want to be cast as a player in this drama."

"You deceive yourself. Or you are the victim of deception. The burden you have assumed can be handed on to one who should rightfully shoulder it."

"I can't make you understand, can I? I have no *choice* in this. Fate has made the decision for me." He paused for a second to let that sink in, then added, "In any event, who is this person you refer to as being the real prophesied champion?"

Hadzor looked offended again. "Why, *me*, of course."

That did it. The alarm bells were deafening now. Leandor was dealing with a madman. "Is this another supposition for which you have no proof?"

"I have circumstantial evidence, a great deal of it. At least as many of the pointers that indicate you are the one the prophecy speaks of apply to me. And I have studied demon lore and the book for years. Grant me an audience and I will explain it all."

Leandor had better things to do than listen to

Hadzor's fantasies. It was time to retreat. "Not now. I'm already late for an important meeting concerning the city's defences."

"When can we speak? Danger threatens. We must act without delay!"

"Look, Hadzor, I'll be frank with you. I know beyond doubt that you cannot be the one referred to by the prophecy. Take my word for it. You have allowed yourself to be ensnared by a … delusion. Can't you see that?"

"What I see is that you want to gain the book for your own ends. You dream of the glory its power will bring you." His face was reddening as his anger swelled. "But you are wrong! Hear me, Dalveen Leandor! Using the book for selfish purposes will lead to destruction! Whereas I would employ it for the well-being of all!"

"For the gods' sake, Hadzor, get a grip! All I'm saying—"

"Sir! *Sir!*"

Leandor broke off as a palace guard waded through the mob.

The man arrived breathless. "We've been looking everywhere for you, sir," he panted. "There is a message from the Princess Bethan. She bids you to come to the King's private quarters with all haste!"

"All right." He turned back to address Hadzor. But he had disappeared. There was no sign of him in the crowd.

Leandor shrugged and put the stranger from his mind.

He started to run in the direction of the palace.

CHAPTER 3

Striding one of Torpoint's main corridors, Leandor met Tycho, who had also been urgently summoned to the King's presence.

As they hastened along together, Dalveen quickly related his bizarre conversation with the man calling himself Drew Hadzor. Despite his original conviction that Hadzor was crazed, for some reason the encounter played on Leandor's mind. Or perhaps telling the homunculus of it was a way of avoiding his concern about the King for a few minutes.

"Do not forget that there has been a great deal of interest in the book since your story became known," Tycho reminded him. "And this Hadzor is not the first to have expressed an opinion on the subject."

"I've been collared once or twice by citizens with theories, it's true. But never before by anyone claiming a greater right to the book."

"I grant that *is* a new twist. It does not make your mysterious petitioner anything more than a crank, however. Particularly as he told you nothing new concerning the prophecy."

"No, he didn't. But there was something about Hadzor; he seemed so damned *sure* of himself."

"I have observed that deranged humans can have powerful personalities, and indeed can be very convincing."

"A lesson you learned during your time in servitude to Avoch-Dar, no doubt?"

"It is a debatable point whether the sorcerer is actually mad, Dalveen. I believe him not to be. Unless extreme evil can be called a form of madness." They were approaching King Eldrick's private apartments. "But I venture to say that now is not the time to discuss such matters."

Leandor nodded grimly.

Princess Bethan met them outside her father's bedchamber.

Keeping vigil night and day with the King had made pale her usually robust complexion. The blueness of her eyes was offset by dark rims beneath. Paths of tears streaked her face.

With a tired gesture she brushed aside a lock of blonde hair before clasping Leandor's outstretched hand.

"He's taken a turn for the worse," she explained. "They say his condition is … grave."

"Is he conscious?"

"Yes, and his mind is quite lucid. He's particularly anxious to speak with you and Tycho. But he's very weak, Dalveen, and we mustn't do anything to overexcite him."

They quietly entered the dimly lit room.

Quixwood was sitting by the bed. A high priest chanted softly. To one side, a trio of physicians huddled together in whispered consultation.

Eldrick was propped up by a mound of pillows. A courageous warrior in his younger days, the passing years and his recent wound had exacted their toll. His hair and copious beard were pure white. The once full, ruddy face had given way to hollow cheeks and taut, sallow skin.

Yet his eyes still held nobility and wisdom.

Focusing on Leandor and Tycho, he managed a feeble smile.

"I desire privacy," he commanded, but his voice held only a portion of its former strength.

Bethan ushered out the doctors and the priest.

Then Tycho asked softly, "How are you, sire?"

"My life draws to a close."

"Father—" Bethan began.

"No, child, pretending otherwise is to deceive ourselves. And you must not despair. I have lived long and achieved much. There are no regrets."

She bowed her head, a hand to her mouth.

"I have no fears concerning my fate," Eldrick continued. "But in contemplating Delgarvo's future, and the fortunes of you all, I find myself troubled."

"How so?" Leandor said.

"Governing a realm is a far from easy task. Put a foot wrong and you risk war with neighbouring states. Ignore the well-being of your own people and you invite discontent, even insurrection."

"We have your example as a guide. That will stop us making such errors."

"Do not misunderstand me, Dalveen. I know I leave the nation in good hands, and perhaps I offend you by speaking as I do. But my time is too short to waste on words of silk."

"What do you wish us to do?"

"First, something I know you will do anyway. Support Bethan. At my death the crown will pass to her. Help your queen, all of you, in keeping the realm stable. Work with her to maintain freedom, and to return prosperity to Delgarvo's subjects." He glanced at Quixwood. "In this you will benefit greatly from heeding Golcar's prudent counsel."

"Thank you, sire," the old warrior responded.

"Likewise, in affairs of state our new friend Tycho has proved invaluable. You would do well

28

to consult him, too."

The homunculus acknowledged the compliment with a simple, "My liege."

"And I say this to you, Dalveen: a queen needs her consort. I hope you will not much longer delay your marriage to my daughter."

Leandor gave a slight nod, but made no comment.

"You will find hard the advice I now offer," the King went on, "for it goes against your nature. But you will never have peace of mind, nor devote yourself to ruling with Bethan, as long as you mourn the loss of your arm." He was growing weary. "You have … suffered … a terrible … injustice. Nevertheless, you … must put it … from your mind."

Bethan gently placed her hand on his brow. "Don't tire yourself, my lord. Rest now."

As he drifted from consciousness, she turned to the others and whispered, "We should let him sleep."

Quixwood, Tycho and Leandor filed out silently.

The priest and the physicians went back into the chamber, relieving Bethan. She joined the others in the corridor. A gloomy mood gripped them all.

"I know what father said is difficult for you to accept, Dalveen," she told him. "But he was right; you have to cast away past events in order that we be prepared to take the reins of power. And I think that will be very soon."

Leandor didn't reply. His thoughts were in turmoil. He saw the sense in the King's words, but couldn't resolve his dilemma. How could he be expected to simply forget the wrong that had been done to him? Or ignore the threat he was sure Avoch-Dar still posed?

His mind filled with images of the sorcerer and the dreadful demons he had conjured.

He thought of the Book of Shadows.

And of Shani Vanya, who accompanied him and Tycho, and the traitor Meath, on the quest to recover the book. She hadn't been seen or heard from since leaving Allderhaven the best part of half a year ago.

A window on the other side of the corridor showed heavy snow falling from the night sky.

Not for the first time, Dalveen felt a small pang of disloyalty to Bethan when Shani came to mind. It wasn't entirely clear to him why. All he knew was that when he remembered her his emotions became ... complicated.

He wondered where she was and how she fared.

CHAPTER 4

If Shani Vanya hadn't stolen the horse she'd have a good mind to demand her money back.

She looked down at the dead animal and cursed her luck.

Night had fallen, and it was bitterly cold. A blizzard was blowing and the snow was already calf-deep. There was no real shelter anywhere in the barren landscape. And she wasn't sure exactly where she was, except that Cawdor lay due north and this was bandit territory.

It was not a good time or place to be without a horse.

Three days before, Shani's previous mount had gone lame. As her wanderings had taken her to the outskirts of a township, there was no trouble finding a fresh one. Naturally she hadn't bothered to consult the owner. But she was careless and had to leave in a hurry, a band of irate citizens on her trail. They only gave up when she entered this lawless region.

Now there were just two options. Stay here and risk freezing to death or try to make her way to Bearsden. Neither was particularly appealing.

Bearsden had to be one of the most dangerous places in Delgarvo. A magnet for brigands, cutthroats and fugitives, it was notorious as a mercenary stronghold.

Shani hated mercenaries.

Facing what she thought was north, she cupped her hands around her eyes and peered into the snowstorm. Through the swirling flakes she made out the distant peaks of mountainous Cawdor. That meant east was to her right. If she went that way she'd reach Bearsden, providing it wasn't too far and the weather allowed her.

She rummaged in the saddlebags for a few small possessions, cramming them into her pockets. Then she checked the leather scabbards she wore beneath her shirt sleeves. Fingering the set of throwing knives strapped to each arm gave her some comfort.

There was a rolled blanket tied to the back of the saddle. She wrapped herself in it and set off.

The cutting wind chilled her to the bone.

Wading through the drifting snow was hard work, and soon she lost all sensation in her feet and hands. Her face stung from the icy battering, her legs ached.

Keeping track of time became a problem in the blinding whiteness, but she estimated two or three hours had passed when she saw a light. She took heart from it and trudged on. After what seemed an eternity the dark outline of a squat building came into view. As she struggled to it, she heard muffled voices, punctuated by bursts of laughter. She'd found a tavern.

If there were other buildings nearby she couldn't see them. Perhaps this inn stood outside the settlement. Not having to venture into Bearsden itself would suit her fine, although she'd got to the point where she was too cold and fatigued to care. Stretching out a numb hand, she pushed open the door.

Light, noise and warmth hit her like a physical blow.

There were at least a score of men inside, and as Shani came in they immediately fell silent. She ignored them. All that interested her was the log fire blazing in a massive hearth at the opposite end of the room. Every eye in the place was on her as she made for it. Casting aside the blanket, she held her hands to the blissful heat, rubbing them together to get the circulation going again.

When she turned to warm her back, she saw they were all staring at her. It was still quiet enough to hear a rat breathe, and the atmosphere wasn't friendly.

"What do you want here?"

She looked to the innkeeper. A broad, muscular man lacking much in the way of hair, he leaned on his side of the serving counter and regarded her with a stern gaze.

Relaxed and slow, she walked over to him. "What people usually want in a tavern," she replied, "a drink. Mulled wine and brandy."

Somebody behind her sniggered.

"And something hot to eat," she added, glancing at a large pot of bubbling stew on the counter.

The innkeeper didn't move. Shani dug out a couple of silver coins and slapped them down in front of him. He grunted, slid them into the pocket on the front of his grubby apron and started on the drink.

Around the room, conversations resumed, but in hushed tones.

Two men stood further along the bar. One was small and ferret-faced, with a vivid scar running down his right cheek. The other was big, muscle-bound and bullnecked. They openly scrutinized her.

"Can I get a horse around here?" she asked, making the question sound as light and conversational as possible.

"You can get anything in yonder Bearsden," scarface told her gruffly. "If you have the money. *Do* you have the money, girl?"

Bullneck took in Shani's slightly boyish, close-cut blonde hair and masculine clothes. "You *are* a girl, aren't you?" he smirked.

Several of the onlookers chuckled ominously.

"No," she said coolly. "I'm a woman. And I can pay for what I need."

The exchange was cut short by the innkeeper thumping a tankard on the counter. He took a glowing poker and plunged it into the wine and brandy mixture, producing a sizzling hiss. When he finished, she downed half the warm toddy in one long draught, relishing the thaw in her innards. Then a wooden platter of stew was shoved in her direction. She turned away from the two surly men on her left and reached for it.

Two more men drifted over to the counter and positioned themselves on her right. They looked no more sociable than the pair to her rear. She let the food be and eyed the newcomers. Equally tall, and each sporting a bushy black beard, they might have been brothers. Like everybody else in the room, they were armed.

If anything, the atmosphere was more tense than when Shani walked in. She was aware of being closely watched.

"Do I know you?" growled beard number one.

"I don't know, do you?" Shani dipped her finger in the stew and licked it. She made a face.

"I've seen you before," the man persisted.

"Lucky you." She lifted her tankard and finished the drink.

"In Allderhaven."

"Is that so?"

"You were with Leandor."

"Who?" she asked innocently, trying to keep her voice even.

"Dalveen Leandor. Nightshade. Don't tell me you haven't heard of *him*."

She shrugged.

The second bearded man spoke for the first time. "Leandor killed one of our comrades," he announced.

"Really?" she responded casually.

"Really. Perhaps you know who I'm talking about."

"They say Nightshade's killed many men."

"The man I'm thinking of was a soldier of fortune. Like us."

Shani was tiring of this inquisition. "A *mercenary*, you mean." She almost spat the word.

"Whatever you want to call us," said beard number one. "His name was Craigo Meath. Does that jog your memory?"

She'd had enough of this. "Yes, it does, now you come to mention it." Her anger was rising, her tone growing frosty. "Meath was a traitor. He'd aligned himself to Avoch-Dar."

"That's a filthy lie!"

"No, it's a fact. If you considered yourselves friends of his I'm surprised you never suspected his treachery."

"It's not so much a question of friendship," the man replied defensively, almost embarrassed at having to use the word. "It's the code of our profession. Harm one and you harm us all."

She stared resolutely into his shifty eyes. "Yes, I imagine friendship is something your kind has little need of. But I'll not argue with you. I just want a horse so I can get out of here."

"There's no *way* you're getting out of here," beard number two promised darkly.

His companion's hand was on the hilt of his sword. Both men were edging closer. At the same time, Shani was aware of movement behind her. She tensed.

And smiled.

"In that case," she said sweetly, "why don't you join me for dinner?"

The duo in front of her had a split second of puzzlement before the scalding stew hit their faces.

Most of it drenched beard one. Both men howled with rage. Beard two drew his sword.

Shani plucked a knife from her flowing sleeve

and threw it hard. It struck below the second man's throat.

He went down, open-mouthed.

Men were moving towards her from all over the room. Swords and daggers were drawn. Beard one was still scooping the mess from his eyes. She spun around.

The pair behind came forward with menacing blades.

Shani crossed her arms, hands sliding into opposite sleeves to pull free two more knives. In the same fluid movement she threw them, lobbing underarm with all her might.

Scarface took his square to the chest. He collapsed, dead weight.

Bullneck looked down stupidly at the knife protruding from his waist. He managed a couple of faltering steps in her direction, then sank to the floor.

As he fell, she snatched his sword and quickly turned.

The first bearded man was rushing at her with a raised dagger.

She swung at him. The blade tip slashed his face. He spiralled away, shrieking.

About seven seconds, she reckoned. *Too long to down only four. The cold must have slowed my reflexes.*

The other men were still converging, but warily now.

Suddenly one of them dashed forward, flaying the air with his rapier.

She stood her ground until he was an arm's length away before side-stepping, jabbing her sword into his ribcage as she went. He grunted, dropped the weapon and doubled over.

There was a high-backed chair beside her. She leapt on to it, and from there up to the counter. The innkeeper made a grab for her legs. A swift kick to the bridge of his nose put him out of the fight.

The remaining men, no less than a dozen, swept to the bar like a scummy wave. Shani brushed against something. Glancing down, she saw it was the cooking pot of seething stew. She brought back her foot and booted the pot from the counter, showering blistering liquid over her attackers. Several of the nearest screamed and covered their faces.

Then she was weaving along the wooden surface, scattering bottles and tankards as she avoided slashing, probing blades. Every few steps she lashed out, her sword whistling over their ducking heads.

She was beginning to think there were too many of them.

A wiry, mean-featured individual clambered on to the counter at its far end. He charged at her. She tugged out a throwing knife and sent it winging towards him. It embedded under the man's right knee.

He gasped, swayed and lost balance, crashing down on to the thugs swarming below.

Shani took advantage of the chaos and jumped. She hit the floor awkwardly, and as she straightened a swordsman blocked her way.

A kiss of steel despatched him.

Panting, she looked for the door, but saw the path obstructed by tables and benches. Four or five brigands were closing in. She chose the line of least resistance and ran to the wall, slammed into it and turned. The door was to her left.

Just too far to reach before they got to her.

They stormed in for the attack. Her blade met theirs. Near enough to feel their fetid breath, she fought close quarter, countering the onslaught with cut, thrust and parry.

Beyond her assailants, the lightly wounded were recovering and moving forward to join in.

She was going to be overwhelmed.

Driven by desperation she scythed a great arc that forced them to retreat a few steps. In the too brief respite that followed she edged to the left, then was stopped again as they surged back.

The door could be on the other side of the world for all the chance she had of reaching it.

As she had the thought, it opened.

If it was more of them she was done for.

From the corner of her eye she had a fleeting impression of the man who entered. He was imposingly tall, straight-backed and ruggedly built. The only other feature that registered was his full grey-tinged beard.

Shani braced herself. But she noticed that one or two of the men she faced also glanced at the new arrival, and showed no recognition. She battled on.

Then the stranger was beside her.

Moving with a speed hard to credit in one of his size, he lunged at her nearest opponent, deftly evading the man's guard. The stranger's ham fist delivered a tremendous blow to the brigand's chin. He flew into the table at his rear, smashing wood and breaking glass. The others backed off, amazed.

She was no less dumbfounded herself.

Two men gathered their wits quicker than the others. They came forward to renew hostilities.

Shani swiftly pitched a knife at one. He dodged. But not fast enough. The blade clipped his ear. He yelled and pressed a hand to the side of his head, face contorted.

The stranger didn't wait for the other to approach. He ran to him, batting his sword aside with a contemptuous swipe from an open palm. Before he could react, the man was lifted bodily and hurled into the group of mercenaries behind him.

As they struggled to right themselves, the stranger grabbed an oil lantern from its bracket.

He threw it with great force at the tangle of furniture in the centre of the room.

It exploded on impact. An enormous sheet of flame erupted.

He headed for the door, shouting, "Come on!"

Shani hesitated.

"Come!" he insisted. "Or burn in this nest of vermin!"

She followed, backing out with her sword in the defensive position.

Flames rapidly spread across the floor, and were already consuming part of the counter. The smouldering timber was starting to give off thick oily smoke. Sparks rose to the ceiling. The men still standing blundered about in bewilderment and fear.

Outside, the cold slapped her. It was still snowing.

She clasped the stranger's arm. "Who—?"

"This way!" he snapped, his tone inviting no discussion. Pulling free of her hand, he strode to a tethered horse. Once he mounted, she clambered up behind him.

As they set off, the inn was blazing. Screams rang out. A human fireball staggered through the open door and collapsed on to the icy whiteness.

Then the tavern was out of sight. A pink glow lit the sky above the trees shielding it.

"Who are you?" Shani demanded of the stranger's back.

"A friend."

"Oh, how silly of me," she retorted sarcastically. "A *friend*. Of course. Funny I don't remember ever meeting you before."

He let out a booming laugh. "All I've heard of you is true, Shani Vanya! I can see why a man like Nightshade would throw in his lot with one so spirited."

She was startled. "Dalveen? You know him?"

"I will be his salvation."

"What? I don't understand. Did he send you?"

The stranger didn't answer. Shani tried again several times, but he kept silent.

Who in Hades is this man? she wondered. *How does he know who I am? And what can he mean about being Dalveen Leandor's salvation?*

They rode on through the storm.

CHAPTER 5

As day shaded into night the old King's journey through life approached its end.

Except for the High Priest's mumbled dirge, the room was silent. In a recess off the dimly lit chamber the physicians stood mute and despondent. Bethan, Leandor and Golcar Quixwood sat by the monarch's bed.

The vigil had lasted many hours. None present expected it to last much longer.

Face etched with sadness, Princess Bethan clutched her parent's hand. His eyes were open, and still held something of their former lustre, but it was fading.

He tried to speak.

The Princess leaned closer and softly whispered, "Yes, father, I'm here. Golcar and Dalveen, too."

His lips trembled.

She moved closer still. "Father, I can't—"

"*Blade...*"

Bethan didn't understand.

"*A ... blade...*"

Leandor and Quixwood exchanged glances. "We know what he wants," Quixwood told her gently. He nodded at Leandor.

Dalveen stood and drew his sword. He carefully laid its hilt across the King's open palm. Eldrick's fingers slowly closed around it. He managed the weakest of smiles.

"*A ... man could not ... want for ... a ... better ... passing.*"

"It is fitting," Quixwood said, his voice heavy with emotion. "In combat or in peace, a warrior should die with a blade in his hand."

The King stirred feebly. His grip on the sword, and Bethan's hand, briefly tightened. "*My ... place,*" he rasped, "*... my ... place at the ... banqueting table in the ... Hall of the ... Gods ... is ... assured.*"

His gaze fixed upon another scene. A scene beyond the chamber and those gathered around him.

Then his eyes closed for the last time in this world.

The Head Physician came forward and took the

King's wrist. After a moment he sadly shook his head.

Quixwood wearily got to his feet and declared with choking throat, "Eldrick of the Lance is dead." Tears began to roll down his cheeks. "Long live Queen Bethan!"

The physicians and the priest echoed him, falling to their knees before her. Quixwood lowered his aged body and knelt with them.

Leandor went to Bethan. She allowed her feelings full rein and began to sob.

He held her tightly.

Hours later, the tempest of emotions spent, Dalveen and Bethan stood alone in Torpoint's Great Hall.

She ran her fingers lovingly along the armrest of her father's empty throne. Her eyes were misty. Leandor had thought she might cry again, but now she seemed in complete possession of herself.

He laid his hand comfortingly on her arm. "He meant everything to me too, you know. Along with Golcar, I always saw him as a father. And few men are blessed with two fathers, let alone two so wonderful."

She favoured him with a smile.

"The King wouldn't have wanted you to be ruled by despair," he added. "You realize that, don't you?"

"Yes, Dalveen, I know." A look of resolve came

into her face. "I'll not give way. For the sake of his memory, and because of the responsibilities I'll have to bear in future. Preparations are already under way for my coronation. As father said, it doesn't do to leave these things unresolved for too long."

"Of course."

"And arrangements must be made for his … funeral."

He nodded sympathetically.

"But, Dalveen," she continued, "remember father's words about a queen needing her consort. I want you beside me to help shoulder the burden of running Delgarvo. Nothing would please me more than for us to hasten our wedding so that we may sit here together." She nodded to the pair of thrones. "You want that too, don't you?"

He was uneasy. "Naturally I do. But…"

"But?"

"There is unfinished business."

"And whom does it concern?"

"I don't understand," he said, puzzled.

"Could it be that you have … someone else on your mind?"

"I can't imagine who you mean."

"No? What about Shani? Does she occupy your thoughts more than I?"

Leandor was taken aback. "No! I mean … I think about her, naturally. We were comrades at arms on my quest for the book. She aided us

47

against the sorcerer. Of course I worry about her well-being. But as a *friend*. Only that."

She looked unconvinced. Leandor was troubled that she could doubt his loyalty, even if his own feelings on the subject had been confused of late. But before he could reassure her further, Bethan cut in with, "So it's past events that still plague you, is it?" She glanced at his vacant sleeve. "That brute Avoch-Dar. And the wretched book. Despite father's advice, you persist in this fixation. You must rid yourself of it!"

The sternness of her attitude further surprised him. "You're not alone in telling me that," he replied hesitantly. "And I find it distressing to go against the wishes of those closest to me. But you must see that my destiny is to fulfil the prophecy passed on by Melva before she died."

"Has it not occurred to you that you may already have done that?" She indicated the Great Hall with a sweep of her arm. "Have you forgotten that in this very chamber Avoch-Dar had his final triumph denied to him?" Her temper was rising. "Isn't that enough for you?"

"There was nothing final about what happened here, Bethan. It was only a setback for the wizard, not a defeat."

"You really believe that?"

"Yes. As long as Avoch-Dar lives, and has control of the Book of Shadows, no one is safe. My part in this drama is nowhere near played out."

"What do you intend doing?" There was a cold edge to her words.

"I must find Avoch-Dar and retrieve the book. Perhaps it will restore my arm. And *then* we could marry, knowing all is well."

"Is there never to be any peace for us?" she sighed.

"Not if we leave the sorcerer unchecked. He commands the power of the book, and is allied with the demons. My gods, Bethan, don't forget that his actions led to your father's wound and sped his end! Nothing matters, not even our wedding, in the face of the threat he poses!"

"So that fiend is more important to you than me and the kingdom?" she flared.

"No, Bethan! But if Avoch-Dar isn't stopped, there won't *be* a kingdom. Or any safe place in this world for mortal men and women!"

"Even if there is some truth in your theory, why should it stop us marrying?"

"Let me speak frankly. As consort to the Queen I could not avoid becoming entangled with governance of the realm. Now is not the time for affairs of state. It would only obstruct my mission."

"Mission? Obsession, you mean."

"It sorrows me that you should speak of obsessions and theories, Bethan. I need your support above all others."

"And I need *yours*!" she retorted bitterly. "I've never needed you more than I do now."

He could see she was near the end of her tether. "Perhaps this isn't the proper time for such a discussion," he soothed. "But I swear I'll aid you as much as I can in your duties."

"In between seeking the sorcerer and the book? And putting yourself in terrible danger? No, Dalveen. You must decide whether you're going to devote yourself to me and Delgarvo or to this madness!"

"Bethan, I—"

"You've not only lost your arm, you've lost your ability to see what this compulsion is doing to you! And those who love you! You're blind, Dalveen! Blind to the abyss that lies in your path!"

She turned and ran to the door.

"Bethan!"

Quixwood came in. She tearfully swept past him.

"My lady?" he called. "What's wrong? *My lady!*"

But she hurried away without replying.

Leandor dashed after her, intending to follow. Quixwood grabbed his arm. "No, boy. Let her be for a while. She has some grieving to do."

"But, Golcar—"

"Leave it. For now." He regarded Leandor's grim aspect. "It was the marriage, wasn't it?"

"Yes. And Bethan's got some insane notion in

her head about Shani. She seemed almost ...
jealous. You can see how things are, can't you,
Golcar? How can I wed her and linger here in the
capital with Avoch-Dar at large? And with myself
incomplete..."

"You *should* marry Bethan. She sorely needs
your help running the kingdom. And as I've said
before, the best thing you can do about Avoch-Dar
and all the rest of that infernal mess is leave it
behind."

"You can't honestly expect—"

"As to Shani," Quixwood ploughed on, "I can't
blame the Princess for being on edge."

"What?"

"Look at it from her point of view, man. You
refuse to be pinned down about the marriage.
Now there's the shock of her father's passing.
She's bound to feel insecure. And in the circumstances perhaps it's only natural she should
suspect there's a rival for her affections."

"That's absurd! It's nothing to do with Shani.
She isn't even *here*. My concern is with the sorcerer,
and the book. It's with trying to bring back my arm
and fulfilling the prophecy! Can't anybody see
that?"

"That's as may be, Dalveen. But we have to take
the world as it is, and bend to our fate."

"That's what I'm *trying* to do, Golcar! I thought
you, of all people, would understand."

"I *do* understand, but it's a question of priorities. You have to—"

The door burst open. Tycho rushed in

"Forgive me, Dalveen, Golcar! But—"

"Here at least is an ally," Leandor said. "Tycho, you agree with me about the peril we still face from Avoch-Dar, don't you?"

"Indeed I do. That's why I'm here. I had reason to visit the chambers he used, and something extraordinary is happening to his spy crystal."

A chill ran up Leandor's spine. "What of it?"

"It … it seems to have *activated*!"

CHAPTER 6

There was no moon. Bright stars shone in the crystal clear, frosty night sky. The boughs of trees looked ghostly under their white burden.

Shani and the stranger had travelled in silence for several hours.

Now the snow had stopped falling and he slowed their mount. They stopped by a copse of tall trees.

"I suggest we camp here for the night," he said.

She slid from the horse. "So you *can* talk. I thought you'd swallowed your tongue!"

He dismounted and tied the reins to a stunted trunk. "There's no point pushing on at this hour. We should try to make ourselves comfortable until morning."

His tone was so calm she found it infuriating.

"What makes you think I'd stay with a man who won't even tell me his name? Or what business he has with me?"

"Patience is a virtue. Exercise it while we make camp and I promise I'll explain everything."

In the middle of the wilderness with no horse of her own, she had little choice but to go along with him.

They collected wood from the foot of trees, where it was protected from the damp. A patch of ground was cleared and a fire built, well away from overhanging branches laden with snow. The stranger threw down blankets and they settled on them by the warming blaze.

"Now I want that explanation," Shani demanded. "Tell me how you know who I am. And who *you* are. And why did you choose to get involved back in that inn?"

He held up his hands and smiled. "All right, all right. Naturally you have many questions, and I'll answer them all." Producing a small silver flask, he took a long drink. After a hearty smacking of lips, he offered it to her. "Tarlian brandy. It'll keep out the cold."

She shook her head impatiently.

He shrugged, returning the flask to an inside pocket of his spacious outer garment, which resembled a poncho with buttons. Then he announced, "My name is Drew Hadzor."

"That means nothing to me."

"No doubt. Nevertheless I need to talk with you, and I want your aid."

"Talk is free. Aid can come expensive."

He seemed a little offended. "Are you not grateful for my help against those mercenaries? Do you not owe me for—"

"Now *look*," she interrupted, "I didn't *ask* you to butt in, Hadzor, or whatever your name is. It was my fight and I don't remember sending invitations. I owe you nothing!"

He responded with his booming laugh. "Ah, that spirit again. Such fire! You must have been a great asset to Leandor on his quest for the book."

She tensed and eyed him suspiciously. "The … book?"

"Yes, Shani. The Book of Shadows. That is my main interest."

In the flickering firelight, there was something unnerving about the expression on his face.

"What interest can you have in that evil tome?"

"I don't think it *is* evil. I believe it can be used for good."

Shani almost laughed aloud. It occurred to her that he might be mad. "That seems a … curious idea," she said carefully.

"Let me explain. There is no disputing that the book has tremendous power. But what is the nature of that power? Perhaps it is like the wind, which can turn a mill to grind corn or blow up a storm that claims lives and destroys property. Then again it could be like the rain. When the heavens open, that can be a gods-send for a farmer's crop, or the ruination of a village flooded. You wouldn't blame the wind or the rain for the destruction they might bring. They are neutral; they can do good or do harm."

"And you think it is likewise with the book?"

"Yes. My belief is that it can be used negatively or positively depending on who controls it." The fire was growing warm, and as he spoke he began loosening his black over-garment.

Intrigued despite herself, Shani responded, "Even if what you say is true, it seems to me it would take a very exceptional person to direct the book's power. It's a terrible risk."

"Avoch-Dar seems to think he can do it. And Leandor managed some measure of control, did he not?"

"Some, yes. But even he came nowhere near mastering it. He certainly couldn't get it to restore his arm."

"*Even* he?" Hadzor was standing, his fingers working down the remaining buttons of his flowing outer coat.

"You must know that Dalveen Leandor has good reason to believe he is a prophesied champion," she told him, "a man whose destiny is entwined with the book."

"I know he *thinks* that, yes. It could be that it is not so. Or that it isn't just him who can cope with the book's power." He pulled out the brandy flask again.

"You're implying there are others?"

"One other."

Perhaps he *was* mad. He was certainly arrogant.

"Oh, I see," Shani mocked. "You think a drunken brawler like yourself might have better luck, is that it?"

At that moment, Hadzor finished unbuttoning his loose poncho. It fell away, revealing distinctive brown and grey clothing beneath.

The significance of his garb wasn't lost on her. It could only mean one thing.

"Come now, Shani," he teased. "Is that any way to speak to a man in holy orders?"

Leandor was first to arrive at the chamber which housed the crystal.

It was at the top of Torpoint's remotest tower, and had served as Avoch-Dar's quarters in his days as Court Magician.

Tycho arrived next, taking the winding stairs swiftly and without noticeable effort. Quixwood's older bones slowed his progress, and he brought up the rear, stiff and breathless.

When all were gathered, Leandor threw open the door.

Few who lived and worked in Torpoint would venture into this place.

Many people remarked on how the chamber seemed always cold, whatever the temperature outside. This night was no exception.

Two or three candles were scattered about. But they were not the main source of illumination. Near the centre of the room, on a solid oak table, stood the enchanted crystal. It was about the same size as a man's head, and multifaceted. By way of its magic, Avoch-Dar had spied on Leandor's quest for the book. When the sorcerer fled, the crystal was left behind, dull and lifeless.

Now a milky whitish glow pulsed deep within it.

There was just enough light to make plain certain marks on the slabs of granite that formed the floor; patterns that hard scrubbing by palace servants had failed to completely erase. The large outline of a five-pointed star, a pentagram, was still clearly visible. Other magical symbols, of intricate and complex design, were also present, their tracings akin to ghostly slug trails on the unyielding stone. They bore testament to hellish rituals the wizard had performed here.

As Leandor, Tycho and Quixwood stared, the swirling luminescence at the crystal's heart grew more intense.

"What does it mean?" Quixwood whispered.

"I don't know," Leandor replied. "But be on your guard."

"Perhaps it would be wisest to summon practitioners of white sorcery," Tycho suggested, "and have them cast protective spells about the gem."

Leandor shook his head. "No. I doubt they could contain its magic. And I want nobody else here. I've waited a long time for this thing to show signs of life."

Sparkling, brightly coloured pinpricks danced inside the pallid cloud. Leandor moved closer.

"Have a care, Dalveen!" Quixwood cautioned, drawing his sword.

Something resembling miniature ribs of lightning flashed in the crystal. Then the churning cloud it held showed tiny, silent explosions, so vivid it almost hurt to look at them.

"Something forms!" the homunculus exclaimed.

The dazzling, agitated mist was taking on a distinct shape. Slowly the wavering image solidified.

It became a man's face.

The stamp of evil and corruption was upon it. Sunken cheeks and taut skin gave a cadaverous impression. The hair and goatee beard were ebony, the complexion olive, overlaid with a sallow, waxy hue.

His eyes were the most disturbing feature. They were black pits. And their gaze was like a predatory beast's.

"*Avoch-Dar!*" Quixwood gasped.

The sorcerer smiled in an unpleasant way. "Greetings, Nightshade," he smoothly intoned. Delivered via the crystal, his voice had an echoey, unreal edge.

"What's this?" the wizard added. "No warm welcome? No applause on my return to the world of men? I could almost believe you aren't glad to see me." His snorting laugh was derisive.

"I never doubted we'd meet again," Leandor replied. "Though I'd hoped it would be in person, rather than in such a cowardly fashion. But that's only to be expected of vermin."

"Temper, temper," Avoch-Dar mocked. "We'll meet in the flesh soon enough, that I promise."

"My blade and I look forward to it. Apart from niceties, is there a point to this farce?"

"Of course. As a loyal subject, naturally I wish to offer my condolences. Losing the King must be almost as painful to you as when I obliterated your arm." The gloating laughter returned.

"Your part in his death is something else you'll pay for."

"You do me too much honour, Leandor. Although it would be agreeable to think I helped hasten Eldrick's end. As I did with his queen."

"*What* did you say?" a shocked Quixwood demanded.

"Oh, you must have realized, surely?" Avoch-Dar responded casually. "The death of Nerissa was my doing. In studying the magical arts I have acquired an extensive knowledge of poisons. If I recall correctly, in her case I used venom from a swamp-dwelling viper."

"But … *why*?" Leandor said. "What could she possibly have done to deserve such a fate?"

"Nothing. I did it because I knew Eldrick would be thrown into despair. It was so much easier gaining his trust in that state, and securing myself a position at court."

"You *swine*!" Quixwood yelled. "Stand aside, Dalveen! I'm going to smash that thing to fragments!"

"That could be unwise," Tycho warned him.

"It would indeed, you old fool," the wizard confirmed. "Try to harm the crystal and it will certainly harm *you*." He grinned cruelly. "But don't let that stop you."

Leandor grasped Quixwood's sleeve. "His aim is to provoke us, Golcar. Be calm."

"Yes, do not give him the satisfaction of pushing you into anger," Tycho agreed.

"Still offering sage advice I see, Tycho," Avoch-Dar said. "I made you well, it seems. I eagerly anticipate … *unmaking* you."

61

"Threats from a distance are one thing," Leandor told him, "carrying them out is another. Name your ground and face me in combat like a man!"

"Don't be a simpleton, Leandor," the wizard sneered. "*I* make the rules. And you hardly came off best when we last did battle." He adopted an ugly grin. "In any event you'll have no time for such adventures, assuming you're still to marry Bethan. As I once nearly did."

"When you tried to force her, you mean."

Avoch-Dar ignored him. "She will make a comely bride. But an even more fetching widow."

"Bluster as much as you like, dog. You still have me to reckon with."

The sorcerer's face grew awful and malignant. "A pathetic cripple will not stand in my way. I will have my revenge on you. If you are sure of nothing else, Nightshade, be sure of that."

Before Leandor could reply the light in the crystal went out like a snuffed candle. The gem returned to its dead, chill state.

All that remained was an impossible pungency in the air.

An aroma very much like sulphur.

chapter 7

"*Y*ou're a *priest*?" Shani was dumbfounded.

"A monk, actually."

"Monk, priest, whatever you call yourself, your behaviour's hardly what one expects of a holy man. Where did you learn to fight like that?"

"I belong to the Brotherhood of the Inner Light," Drew Hadzor announced proudly. "We are an ancient order of warrior monks."

"I've heard of them. But I thought the order died out long ago."

"No, we merely withdrew from the world to undertake our devotions in peace. We are modest in numbers, but still active in the remoteness in which we dwell. As to our ability with the martial arts, that dates back several centuries to a time when we were persecuted and had to defend ourselves. We believed that in doing so we served the will of the gods. The tradition of learning fighting skills has continued, but more these days as a discipline."

"So it's your brotherhood that seeks the Book of Shadows?"

"Not exactly."

She raised an eyebrow.

"But they know of my interest in it," he hastily added. "It's just that I'm not here ... officially."

"They don't approve of your little adventure."

"Suffice to say our Abbot has his doubts about the wisdom of my quest. But think, Shani! Think of all the good I could do with the power the book confers!"

"Leaving aside your theory about that for a moment, consider the practicalities. One problem we had was that we couldn't even *understand* the book. Its words were a mystery to us."

"That wouldn't be as great a problem for me. My order has preserved examples of the demon race's written language, which I've studied extensively. That's how I became interested in them and their book in the first place. There aren't many surviving fragments of their writings, but I'm sure I could make sense of the tome."

Above the distant horizon the sky was blood red. Dawn was beginning to break.

"All right," Shani said. "Second problem. And this you may not be aware of. The book proved to be so dangerous that simply handling it was no straightforward task. It killed its own *guardian*, a being called Kreid, just because he came into contact with it."

The monk frowned. "You're right, I didn't know that. But presumably Nightshade was able to handle it. And Avoch-Dar took it, so—"

"Leandor seemed to be the only one who could touch the book without harm. But that's due to his destiny being entwined with it."

"So you say."

She disregarded his scepticism. "And Avoch-Dar didn't actually touch it himself. He was very careful not to, in fact. It was taken by one of the demons he conjured, and with whom he disappeared through a ... a kind of magical gateway."

Hadzor considered that for a moment, then stated, "I still think it's a question of knowing how to master the book properly. A case of applying the correct knowledge."

"That's hardly something you can learn through trial and error."

"I'll find a way around it."

She thought him either very determined or very stubborn. Probably both. "We'll let that pass, too," she decided. "What you haven't considered, of course, is the biggest problem of all: the fact that

Avoch-Dar and the book aren't in this world any longer."

"Oh no, Shani, I'm sure you're wrong about that. Avoch-Dar is almost certainly in this world. He may have spent some time in the demons' dimension, but—"

"*What?* How can you be so sure?"

"I have no magical abilities myself, but an elite within my brotherhood does. The Order of the Inner Light is custodian to a wealth of secret lore, and those initiated to the highest ranks of the fraternity are masters of white sorcery. Several months ago, they felt a tremendous disturbance in the invisible web that binds all life, and to which they are psychically attuned. Their interpretation of this event was that Avoch-Dar had left the realm of demons and could be back in Pandemonium."

Mention of the city the wizard had magically created for himself in Vaynor sent a chill up Shani's spine. Rare accounts from those who had seen it and lived told of a sort of necropolis; a place of hideous aspect, more suited to the dead than the living.

"I'd like to think your order is wrong about that," she told him. "I for one hoped we'd seen the last of him and that infernal book."

"The book *can* be used for good, Shani, believe me. And help me find it."

"How do you think I can help you? Or that I'd want to get involved in such an insane scheme?

The book's *deadly*, man! Anyway, if what you say is true, it's to be found in Vaynor."

"I was hoping you might have some kind of clue or information that could be useful to my search. As to why you should help, my knowledge of the demons' language would be invaluable. If I could control the book, I might be able to aid Leandor in regaining his arm."

"*Might* is the word. You'd be going against Avoch-Dar, assuming he *is* back in Vaynor, and that's something I'd think twice about doing."

"Sooner or later the sorcerer has to be confronted, Shani. Because he isn't going to rest until he's conquered Delgarvo. And everywhere else!"

"Dalveen believes that too, and I expect you're both right. Come to think of it, why didn't you go directly to him?"

"I did go to him. I spent a week trying to convince Allderhaven bureaucrats to grant me an audience. In the end I was reduced to accosting him in the street."

"And what did he say?"

"Leandor is a warrior of incomparable courage, of that there is no doubt. In the matter of the book, however, he has obviously allowed his judgement to be clouded."

Shani thought that was rich coming from Hadzor, but only said, "You mean he wouldn't listen to you?"

The monk ignored her jibe, or didn't recognize it as one. "I fear his quest for glory has got the better of his good sense. He would not consider my argument that he might not be the book's rightful custodian."

She couldn't restrain herself any longer. "I'm not surprised, Hadzor! How would *you* feel if confronted by someone insisting that your destiny is a sham, but offering no proof to back the argument? The man you speak of is not the Leandor *I* know. He doesn't seek glory and his judgement is as clear as anyone I've ever met."

"Let us agree to disagree on that," the monk responded indignantly. "My point is that Leandor has a part to play in recovering the book. That's why I want to recruit him to my cause."

"*Your* cause?"

Again, he disregarded her. "So I am still prepared to present my case to him, and thought that if you put in a word for me—"

"*Look!*" she interrupted, pointing out across the snowy plain.

With an expression of ill grace, Hadzor snapped back to reality and followed her gaze.

A group of riders, black dots against the rising sun, were advancing their way. They were too far off to make out their number.

"I suppose it would be wildly optimistic to assume they're friendly?" Shani remarked.

"A group of mercenaries from Bearsden, I'll warrant, out for revenge."

"Do we stand and fight or make a run for it?"

"The pair of us are never going to outrun them on one horse."

"That's what I thought." She pulled up a sleeve, revealing her sheath of throwing knives. "Need one of these?"

Hadzor slipped a hand into his robe. It emerged bearing a farming implement Shani had seen other fighters use as a makeshift weapon: two short clubs, the tops of each joined by a length of chain. A rice flail. "I find this serves me well enough," he told her.

The riders, galloping at speed, were much nearer now. There were four of them.

"They have the advantage of being mounted," Hadzor stated. "Facing them on foot is bad strategy. Perhaps one of us should take my horse."

She glanced to his mount, then back at the advancing group. "No time. Prepare to make a stand!" They spread out.

The riders were close enough for Shani to see that they were dressed entirely in black. Their costume matched the colour of the horses.

"They're not mercenaries," she realized.

The two leading horsemen were well ahead of the others. The pair split, one making for Shani, his companion for Hadzor.

She snatched a knife and braced herself. From the corner of her eye she saw that, like her, the monk was motionless. She guessed that he too would wait until the final second before acting.

Returning attention to her own opponent, she watched as he bore down, sword pointing like a lance. Standing firm, she drew back her arm and quickly assessed the target. She took into account the speed he moved at, and the angle of throw necessary to hit him.

Then she lobbed the blade.

It slammed into his chest. The impact knocked him back, sword flying from his hand. His body whiplashed and slumped forward again, head drooping. Shani sprang aside and the unguided horse thundered past, the corpse bouncing in its saddle.

Hadzor nimbly side-stepped as his foe approached and expertly flipped one end of his flail up at the rider. The club and chain wrapped around the horseman's sword arm. Momentum and a sharp tug did the rest.

The man yelled and crashed from the mount. He struck the ground hard and didn't move again. His horse shied and kept galloping.

Shani and Hadzor had no time to savour their victory. The two remaining riders were upon them.

She was lucky to avoid the blade of the one who came at her. It passed near enough for her to feel the air it displaced. Her assailant rode by, pulled on his reins and turned for another charge.

Hadzor was dodging sword strokes from his new antagonist. Several swipes came uncomfortably close to parting his head from his body. But the monk's agility paid off. One club of the flail in each hand, he managed to loop the chain over the saddle's pommel. Then he pulled with all his might, and in an incredible display of strength, downed man *and* horse.

The terrified animal righted itself and bolted. Its rider quickly scrambled to his feet and set about Hadzor with his sword. The monk deftly fended the blows, but seemed unable to find an opening in his foe's defences.

It took all of Shani's swiftness to escape being trampled by her attacker's second charge. Her man circled and made ready for a third. She couldn't elude him for ever. There had to be a way to end this, and end it quickly. Noticing a fallen tree nearby gave her an idea of how to do it.

She glimpsed Hadzor's fight. The swordsman was slashing wildly at him, and as she watched, his blade clipped the monk's chest. Hadzor staggered from the force of the blow. Somehow he stayed on his feet.

Shani had problems of her own. The rider was sweeping towards her. She left it as long as she could before running for the tree trunk. All was nearly lost when, ten paces into her dash, she slipped and almost lost balance. Then she was at the trunk. She leapt on to it and spun around.

Just in time to duck as the man's whistling blade barely cleared her head.

The trunk gave her the extra height she needed. As the man struggled to hold steady his horse, she half stretched, half jumped and scrabbled up behind him.

Before he could turn she plunged her knife between his shoulder-blades.

She toppled him from the saddle, grabbed the reins and sped to Hadzor.

Before she covered the short distance, he was besting his opponent. He had the man in a bear-hug, gripping him from the rear. The chain of the flail was around the man's throat and he'd dropped his sword. Hadzor gave the chain a single, twisting jerk. There was a crack. The man spasmed and sank lifeless to the ground.

Shani dropped from the horse. Hadzor's hand was against his chest. He wore a pained expression.

"Are you all right?" she asked.

He reached inside his robe. "Damn!"

"Is it bad?"

"I'll say it is!" He brought out the flask. It was punctured, brandy seeping from the gash. He licked his fingers and grumbled inaudibly.

Relieved, she laughed, and tied the horse's reins

to a tree. Then she knelt to look at the man Hadzor had just finished.

The monk joined her and scrutinized the corpse's black garb. "You're right, these are no mercenaries."

Shani noticed the glint of a silver chain at the dead man's neck. She slipped it from his jerkin. It supported a fist-sized medallion in the shape of a five-pointed star enclosed in a circle.

"A pentagram," Hadzor said.

"And I'll wager they're all wearing one."

"What do you make of it?"

"I think they're Avoch-Dar's men."

"They're a long way from Vaynor. Sent for us, do you think?"

She shuddered. "Looks like it, doesn't it?"

"It seems I was right about the sorcerer coming back. Perhaps you're set to tangle with him again whether you like it or not, Shani."

"Not alone. Leandor should be told about this immediately."

"Return to Allderhaven, you mean? And you'll speak to him on my behalf?"

"Yes." Mentally she crossed her fingers. She'd meant yes to his first question, no more than a maybe to his second. "Come on, we should get away from here without delay. There may be more of them." She went off to gather her possessions.

Hadzor stared at the pentagram for a moment. Then snapped it from its chain.

CHAPTER 8

An image of Drew Hadzor's perplexed face floated on the surface of the pool. Viscous yellow-green liquid churned around it.

Avoch-Dar peered down intently at the monk's features.

Then Hadzor took hold of the pentagram and wrenched it from its chain. Instantly his likeness disappeared.

"Damnation!" the sorcerer roared.

Roughly the same diameter as the wheel of a large ox cart, the pool was set flush to the floor. Avoch-Dar stood by a low bulwark encircling it, and watched as the swirling emerald fluid began to calm. He raised his hands and conjured a spell. A small cluster of bubbles appeared on the now placid surface, popped feebly and sent out tiny ripples. But he couldn't bring back the image, or establish contact with the pentagrams his other three agents wore.

His link with the medallions depended on the life energy of the wearers. Only death would break the connection, and the life of the man whose medallion he'd just seen ripped away must have been near over. He must have expired as the chain was broken.

He should have known better than to send just four against Shani Vanya. But she would pay dearly for it next time. And whoever her companion was, he too would regret his interference.

Avoch-Dar's palace stood at the heart of Pande-monium. It was larger, higher and more grotesque in appearance than any of the other strange, contorted buildings making up his capital in Vaynor.

The massive Great Hall in which he stood was fashioned entirely from black marble. Huge pillars of the same material, patterned with overlays of alabaster, soared up to support its distant vaulted ceiling, hidden in darkness far above. Light came from guttering torches in iron brackets.

Avoch-Dar was near one end of the cavernous room. To his right, perhaps fifty paces away, there was an entrance to a further, smaller chamber.

It was unlit. A cave of shadows.

The atmosphere inside was misty, almost a fog, per-meated with a foul smell resembling sulphur. And there were noises. They were hushed and low, and unlike any sound made by man or beast.

Shapes moved within, the meagre light only hinting at their true nature. They were distorted, askew, inhuman forms. Beings from a nightmare.

One detached itself and came towards him.

It could not be said that it walked. Nor did it pad, crawl, slither or drag its bulk across the marble floor. Its movements combined all these things, and it left a trail of glistening slime.

The wizard turned to look at the creature. If forced to describe it, he would have had difficulty finding the words. It was much taller than him. In equal parts insect, reptile, carnivorous feline, there was something about it which also reminded him of the webbed and scaly life-forms that inhabited the ocean's depths.

Despite its appearance, the creature's many eyes shone with an acute intelligence. But cruelty, ruthlessness and a terrible kind of hunger were there, too. Even Avoch-Dar had to steel himself when meeting their savage gaze.

"I trust all is to your satisfaction, Berith?" he enquired of the demon lord.

"Not entirely." Its voice was a throaty, sucking grunt. It gave the impression it wasn't used to something as primitive as speech.

The sorcerer ignored the gust of foul breath that swept into his face. "What displeases you?" he asked.

"We too observed the failure of your action against

the female. This does not inspire confidence among the Sygazon." It pronounced the name of its race with a somewhat higher, louder intonation, as though to emphasize its importance. "What purpose is served by attacking Nightshade's associates? How does it contribute to the campaign against him?"

"Killing Leandor's friends deprives him of allies and further crushes his spirit."

"Had you been successful."

Avoch-Dar's features hardened with indignation. "The men I sent turned out to be fools. In any event, they were only directed to Vanya and her companion because they happened to be in the area."

"So it was not so much a plan as a whim."

"No! An opportunity arose to strike at our enemies and I seized it."

"You mean you saw a chance for revenge against one of those who had thwarted you. Acting on impulse is not always the wisest path to follow, Avoch-Dar."

"I see no wrong in exacting revenge. As for impulse, that has always been my way. Nothing is gained by waiting for chance to deal a winning hand. One must act!"

"But not at the risk of ruining everything. If you wish to achieve dominance in this world concentrate your efforts on Nightshade. He is the single biggest threat to your ambitions. And to the Sygazon's purpose here."

"I grow impatient with talk of your purpose."

"Why?" the demon rasped.

"Because I know next to nothing about it! When we sealed our pact and came through the dimensional portal to Vaynor, you agreed to increase my magical powers. You offered me mastery of the book in exchange for my aid. You made many promises, but few have been honoured."

Berith's hideous face was unreadable.

"It is time you told me more of your scheme," Avoch-Dar went on.

"We want what you want: the destruction of Nightshade."

"That can be only part of your design."

"True, although a vital part."

"And the rest of your scheme?"

"Will unfold in due course."

"I could almost suspect that there is some reason why you need others to carry out your bidding," Avoch-Dar ventured slyly, "a reason you are not anxious to reveal. Could it be that there is a limit to your powers in this world?"

This struck a nerve, and the demon lord responded with a disapproving hiss. Its scaly chest visibly swelled. The implied threat in the gesture was unmistakable. "The Sygazon admit of no limits to their capabilities. Our plans will be revealed to you when the time is judged right."

Berith's cat and mouse game was inciting the sorcerer's anger. He tried a different tack. "Do I have to remind you that it was I who allowed you back into this world via the pentagram at Torpoint? Does that not entitle me to an explanation?"

"Correction," the demon growled. "You used the book to bring that about. And you needed our intervention to escape Nightshade."

"Had I not plotted to obtain the book in the first place, and employed my sorcery in its use, you would not be here now!"

"And neither you nor we could have returned from our dimension without the Sygazon's greater knowledge of the book. Fate has bound us together, Avoch-Dar. To accomplish our aims we must work in partnership."

The wizard was no nearer knowing what he could do for the Sygazon that they couldn't do for themselves. He gazed at Berith, and beyond the demon lord to the others of its kind, milling in their hole of darkness. Not for the first time he mused on whether his magic was more powerful than theirs, and which side would emerge victorious should it be put to the test. He was tempted to find out. Then he looked into the demon's multitude of flinty eyes and decided against it. For now.

"I need to master the book," he said. "At least help me to command its magic."

"Its power is beyond imagining," Berith hissed. "Control is no easy matter, particularly for a mortal. Be patient and we will open its secrets to you."

Patience was not one of Avoch-Dar's strong points, but he had no choice other than to bide his time.

79

He looked to the centre of the enormous hall. A structure of black obsidian stood there. It could be mistaken for an altar. The uppermost slab of the imposing edifice bore just one object. An object that gave off an eerie blue luminescence.

The Book of Shadows.

Dalveen and Bethan remained at Eldrick's funeral pyre until the flames turned to embers. Then he had persuaded her to return to Torpoint.

He chose a drawing-room in the palace that overlooked the funeral site and left her in peace as she gazed down at the snowy scene.

At length he gently took her arm and said, "Come away now."

She allowed herself to be guided towards a seat in front of the room's blazing log fire. They spoke of her father, and tears came to her again.

After a while spent in silence, and with her sadness in check, Bethan regained something of her old spirit.

"I think I owe you an apology," she sniffed. "About Avoch-Dar."

"No, you don't. I should seek *your* forgiveness for telling you about his visitation on the eve of your father's funeral. But you had to know about it, Bethan, it's too important to pretend it didn't happen."

"Of course. Nevertheless I was wrong. I thought

... well, *hoped* really, that we would never see him again. But you were right all along. He's back. And the things you told me he said..."

"His gloating at your father's death, yes. And his boast about your mother." He squeezed her hand. "There's a good chance he said that only to wound."

"I know. But it has the ring of truth, doesn't it, Dalveen? Even if it was a lie, it shows the depth of the man's wickedness."

"There was never any doubt about that. But doesn't it strike you as strange that Avoch-Dar should be sending threats rather than acting?"

"Perhaps he *is* acting. He could be hatching all kinds of plots we're unaware of. There is another possibility though."

"What's that?"

"Suppose he hasn't full control of the book. That would explain why he's merely threatening you via the crystal instead of standing at our gates again."

"That's possible," Dalveen replied thoughtfully. "But he's allied to the demons, or presumably he is. Wouldn't they teach him its proper use?"

"There could be something preventing that. Then again, if the demon race is as powerful as everyone says, why do they need the sorcerer? What can he have to offer them?"

"My feeling is that he must be of value to them or he wouldn't still be drawing breath. I'm also more convinced than ever that he's no longer in their dimension. He's here somewhere, in our world."

"I was coming to the same conclusion, although the thought troubles me. As does knowing that the wizard is a formidable enough opponent even *without* the book."

"There's no denying that. We must be vigilant."

"What happens now?"

"I don't know."

"Will you be leaving me? Are you going to search for the sorcerer?"

"I haven't worked it out. But if I have to go, I promise it won't be for long."

She looked doubtful, and a little frightened.

"Let's not speak of this today of all days," he said.

Bethan nodded.

"And there are more mundane chores to attend to," he went on. "For instance, we apparently have a visitor, according to a message Tycho sent. Someone he's quite insistent we should see."

"Who is it?"

"I've no idea. Would you mind if I summoned them? If Tycho thinks it's important—"

"Yes, of course. Send for them now."

Leandor walked to the bell-pull and tugged it twice.

Shortly after, the homunculus entered. He had a woman with him.

She was young. Her hair was auburn, her skin clear and hazel eyes bright. She was tall and quite thin. There was about her an air of self-assurance, despite her youth, and the smile she favoured them with was warm and genuine.

"This is Karale," Tycho said.

The girl bowed. "Thank you for seeing me." Her voice was soft and melodic. "And my condolences on your loss, Princess. His Majesty will be sorely missed."

"You are kind," Bethan quietly replied.

"I'm sorry, er, Karale," Leandor interjected, "should I know you?"

"We have not met before. But I bear a family likeness to someone you have known."

"There is something familiar about your features…"

"I'm told I have inherited my grandmother's looks. You knew her as Melva."

Leandor was startled. "You are kin to Melva? The wise woman?"

"Yes. And I am pleased to meet you at last, Nightshade." She smiled. "You look surprised."

"Well, yes," he admitted. "I suppose it never occurred to me that Melva had relatives."

"Of course she did," Karale laughed. "Do you not recall her telling you that the prophecy of which she was custodian was handed down through the generations?"

"Yes. But surely, having passed it on to me—"

"Had the time not been right, that could have been my task. Or my daughter's, or her daughter's."

"Have you come to add more to the prophecy?"

"Not exactly. I'm sorry, I can see that you are disappointed. But I think the service I am here to render will prove useful to you."

"I don't understand."

"You will. I need just a small portion of your time. And a private place in which to do what must be done."

"If you are truly Melva's granddaughter that is the least I can do for you. Do you wish for us to be alone?"

"That is not necessary."

"And will these chambers serve your needs?" Bethan added.

"Perfectly. But I need a brazier of hot coals. And could you close the shutters on that window?"

"Would you have that attended to, Tycho?" Leandor asked.

The homunculus nodded and hurried to fetch servants.

"Is there anything we must do to assist you in this mysterious enterprise, Karale?" Leandor said.

"Just be seated. As I said, what I must do will not delay you long."

In a matter of moments the brazier was in position and the shutters bolted. The door was secured. At Karale's request, no candles were lit.

She took a variety of small containers from the leather shoulder bag she wore and placed them on a table next to the brazier. Tycho enlivened the coals with hand bellows before joining Dalveen and Bethan on a semicircle of chairs.

"It seems you are about to engage in some kind of conjuration," Bethan observed. "Will you assure us it holds no peril for this place, or any within it?"

"Trust me, Princess. The experience may well seem ... strange, but it holds no danger."

Dalveen exchanged a wary glance with Tycho, then laid his hand upon the hilt of his sword.

"What you are about to see is not a trick," Karale assured them. "It requires my concentration, and that certain things be done in the right order. Please bear with me."

She stared silently into the glowing coals for a few seconds. Then she took up the containers one by one, sprinkling their powdered contents on the coals. Each brought forth a flurry of different coloured sparks, acrid smoke and pungent odours.

As she did this, Karale began quietly half chanting, half singing the words of a ritual in a tongue none of them recognized. Before long her eyes became trance-like. A fine sheen of perspiration dampened her forehead.

Despite the brazier, and blazing fire in the hearth, the room grew noticeably cooler. Bethan shivered and moved close to Leandor. He and the homunculus tensed.

A faint, almost undetectable sound could be heard. It might have been an echo of the incantation Karale recited. Or other voices chanting a different dirge. Perhaps it came from some unknown musical instrument. Again, it could have been the distant, keening wind.

Something happened just above the floor in the middle of the room. A section of the air seemed to turn in on itself. Straight as a die, a vivid purple slash appeared in the air.

"Dalveen?" Bethan whispered, her fingers cutting into his arm.

Karale, her ritual completed, stared at the manifestation too. She seemed calm.

The gash wavered, stretched and suddenly widened.

Blinding white light exploded from it.

Bethan cried out, and they all shielded their eyes. Except the girl, who continued to stare, unperturbed.

The crack in the air opened more and more. But as it did so the light beyond became easier to tolerate.

Darker than the surrounding radiance, a shape could be seen.

Leandor blinked, trying to make sense of the apparition.

Then, framed by the hazy edges of the wound in reality, it flowed into the room.

Slowly, uncertainly, Leandor rose.

The shape came into focus. Its appearance was clear to him.

"Melva?" he whispered.

CHAPTER 9

There was nothing spectral about the figure standing before them. She seemed to be made of flesh and blood just like any other living human. Physically there was no difference to the way she looked when Leandor last saw her. She still appeared immensely old, with a frail body and skin like brittle parchment.

But there had been a subtle change. She gave out a kind of invisible radiance, an impression of vigour and serenity that had not been present in the last hours of her life.

"Greetings, Nightshade." She smiled benevolently.

He was too taken aback to respond.

The ancient dead woman nodded respectfully to Bethan. "Well met, my lady."

Equally dumbfounded, the Princess was lost for words. Tycho, when likewise addressed, managed to acknowledge her with a slight inclination of his head.

Melva regarded her granddaughter. What passed silently between them was unfathomable.

The fissure through which the old woman had entered the world of the living hung in the air behind her. Light pulsating from within the elongated oval was gentler now, yet strong enough to illuminate the chamber and cast shadows of everyone present.

Everyone except Melva.

Leandor found his tongue. "Melva, you're ... dead. *Aren't* you?"

"Yes, Dalveen, I am. Yet not entirely finished with life."

"How can that be?"

"I am trapped in the Realm of Shades, a limbo separating your world and the one beyond. I would not be conversing with you now were it not for Karale. It takes a great effort of will to force open the door between life and death."

"How is it that you find yourself in this state?"

"Until the conflict between Good and Evil has been resolved, I am unable to pass on to a higher plane. And it is far from being resolved."

"But you have played your part here. You *should* have moved on."

"So I thought. It seems Fate has not done with me." She smiled, and this time there was something almost mischievous about it. "Being dead is by no means bad; it tends to clarify one's view of life. It has sharpened my comprehension of the intrigues surrounding you, Dalveen, and of the workings of the prophecy."

"You have more to tell me about it?"

"A little. The ways of Light and Darkness are complex and hard to reckon. Understanding comes slowly. But I tell you this: Avoch-Dar could have access to a power that will bring the world of humans to its end."

"*Could* have?"

"I cannot define the nature of his relationship with the infernal demon race, which incidentally I now know has a name. They call themselves the Sygazon. But it remains a mystery whether he is their master or they his. How much knowledge, if any, they have passed to him is too difficult for me to comprehend."

"Bethan and I have speculated on that point ourselves," Leandor told her.

"You must assume the worst and not be complacent. Even a scrap of demon lore could increase his magical abilities a thousandfold."

"I stand ready," he replied grimly. "Although I confess it would be useful to have a good practitioner of sorcery on our side. But as yet I have found no one who comes near equalling Avoch-Dar in ability. Nor would another few thousand men at arms be unappreciated."

"Take heart," Melva told him. "You may not be alone in your task."

"What do you mean?"

"I am not entirely sure. It is so hard to explain the clarity death brings. But I feel the … *presence* of another form of life, another race; call it what you will. I believe they oppose the Sygazon, and are perhaps of equal strength, yet morally they are opposite. I cannot tell you more."

Leandor glanced at his companions. Bethan remained transfixed by the scene. Tycho's expression was unreadable. Karale's face showed only a kind of tranquillity.

"And there could be aid of a more substantial nature," the old woman continued.

"How so?" he asked.

"My enlightened state has revealed one shard more of the prophecy. It concerns a weapon. A very special … device, that could greatly help you in facing the wizard and the Sygazon."

"Tell me of it, Melva, and where it is to be found."

"I know nothing of its capabilities or location. All I can say is that it may not even appear to be a weapon."

"You speak in riddles."

"Sorry, Dalveen. That is all I have to offer."

"Well, if I ever find the thing," he sighed, "let's hope I take better care of it than I did the Book of Shadows."

"Do not torment yourself with what might have been. There is still everything to be fought for. Nor should you despair at my inability to impart more than I have. The strands of fate are complex indeed, and I have yet to perceive all their ramifications. But know that what I tell you, no matter how puzzling it seems, will prove of value." Melva stopped and turned briefly to the glowing vortex behind her, as though responding to a call they couldn't hear. Smiling, she said, "Prepare yourselves. Another approaches."

Leandor was not alone in being baffled by her words. But before anyone could say anything they saw a shape forming in the shining gash.

Initially the new figure was indistinct. Then it suddenly took on solidity.

Bethan leapt to her feet and cried, "*Father!*"

Like Melva, the late King looked as he had in life, except that the pain had gone from his features. He beamed at his daughter.

She made to run to him, but Eldrick held up a hand. "Forgive me, my dear," he said soothingly. "You cannot touch me. Despite appearances, there is no substance to what you are seeing."

The Princess's face was ashen with shock. Softly, she repeated, "*Father...*" Leandor put his arm around her shoulders.

"Do not despair, Bethan," King Eldrick reassured her. "Melva and Karale are remarkable women. Somehow they have made it possible for us to see each other. Be joyful, not sad."

She bit back the welling tears and asked, "Are you ensnared in the Realm of Shades too, sire?" There was anxiety in her voice.

"No. I am … passing through. And I have but a fleeting moment in which to be with you. But know this, daughter. You are strong. Remember all I have taught you about the art of ruling, trust your instincts, and you will make a fitting queen."

"I will try, father."

The King turned his gaze to Leandor. "It seems you were right about Avoch-Dar, Dalveen. All I'll say is that there is no shame in fearing him, even respecting him a little, for the wizard and that hellish horde are the most formidable enemies you will ever face."

"I do not doubt it, Your Majesty."

"And expect to encounter dangers unconnected to the sorcerer. It would be a shame if you perished at the hands of common rogues before going against him."

"As if I didn't have enough to worry about. Can you tell me the nature of these dangers?"

"That's something you'll have to find out for yourself. But remember that you've made plenty of enemies other than Avoch-Dar, some of them powerful. There's many a brother looking to avenge the sibling you've slain, or an outlaw clan deprived of its leader by your blade. Watch out for yourself, boy."

"This must end now," Melva interjected. "Be ever alert, Dalveen Leandor, and remember what I said about the weapon."

"Father?" Bethan cut in. "Will I speak with you again?"

"Not this way. But eventually, my love, eventually."

The vortex began to throb more intensely.

"I bid you farewell and good fortune," the King added. "And be warned, all of you, that storm clouds are gathering. If Evil is allowed to prevail, these could be Humanity's last days…"

The sound heard earlier, the eerie, haunting lilt of an unknown instrument, returned. It seemed to beat a rhythm in time with the pulsating radiance.

Then the gateway between worlds expanded like a gaping jaw and enveloped Melva and the King.

A dazzling blast of light flooded the room.

And was instantly snuffed out.

It left its glare imprinted on their eyes as they came to terms with the restored gloom. The vortex had disappeared.

Tears were coursing down Bethan's cheeks. "Gods, Dalveen, I—" She broke off and looked about the chamber. "Where is Karale?"

"She was here just a second ago," Leandor said. "Did she pass you, Tycho?"

"No." The homunculus went to the door. "This is still locked," he reported. "And look," he pointed at the table, "her bag and magical paraphernalia have gone, too."

There was nowhere for the girl to conceal herself, and the shutters remained firmly bolted.

"But it's impossible," Bethan whispered.

"If we've learned one thing these past months," Leandor remarked, "it's that the word impossible should be used with caution!"

CHAPTER 10

Shani and Hadzor wasted no time heading south.

Although the cold was still biting, the new day brought better weather. And now Shani had her own horse, so they made good progress as the morning wore on. They saw no one else.

For several hours they had skirted the great northern forests. Soon they would reach the rolling lower plains, and beyond that, the road which eventually led to Allderhaven.

Shani found her companion a little easier to talk to, despite his stubborn attitudes, and they had spoken of many things as they rode. But their conversation always returned to the same subject.

"There's something I don't understand about the book," she said. "Well, there are *many* things I don't understand about it, but one thing in particular has troubled me from the start. Given your knowledge of it, perhaps you have the answer."

"What's the question?"

"Why didn't the demons take the book with them when they left this world for ... wherever it was they went? What was the point of leaving it here?"

"Ah, yes. That problem has long exercised my mind, too. I have no answer, Shani."

"Oh."

"But I do have two theories."

"I thought you might."

"First, they *couldn't* take the book with them."

"Why not?"

"This is all speculation on my part, you understand."

She nodded. "Of course."

"I think it possible that whether they intended it or not, they created something which perhaps even they don't fully understand. Or can entirely control."

"Hmm. It's an interesting thought. But I don't know if I swallow the idea of the book being beyond the demon's control. Although what you say about it having some sort of life fits in with the ... I don't know, the *atmosphere* it generated. It had a kind of presence. Almost like an intelligence. Just being near the thing made me uneasy, to be honest."

"Fascinating. I think that goes some way towards confirming my feelings about the tome. It is more than a mere book. Much, much more…" He drifted into a reverie.

"You said you had two theories," she reminded him.

"Er, yes. The other possibility is that the demons always intended returning and taking the book back. It could be that it still being here is in some way critical to another, grander plan they have."

"Or might it be a sort of key that had to be left behind in order for them to return from their dimension?"

"Perhaps. I don't know. One thing studying what's left of demon lore has taught me is that their culture is totally alien to ours. It isn't easy trying to make sense of their thought processes."

"Leandor may have some theories of his own on that subject. You should talk to him about it. And it could be worth speaking with Tycho."

"Tycho?"

"An homunculus, a being created by Avoch-Dar. He escaped and ended up in Zenobia. We ran into him there and he joined our search for the book."

"Yes, I recall hearing that you were accompanied

on your quest by a magical creature of some sort."

"Tycho proved a valuable comrade. He told us things about Avoch-Dar we hadn't known. And he played a key role in thwarting the wizard's invasion of Delgarvo. He even has a limited form of magical power that proved useful."

"What kind of power?"

"He can levitate objects. There was at least one occasion when I was glad of that."

"This Tycho is in Allderhaven?"

"He was when I left. So that's another good reason to accompany me there."

"A far better reason than merely conversing with Leandor, I think."

She was surprised by the comment. "What do you mean?"

"Well, let's face it, Shani, if Leandor's the hero everyone seems to think he is, he would never have let the book out of his grasp. I'm beginning to wonder whether I have much to learn from him."

"That's not fair, Hadzor!" she flared. "You know nothing of it! We were lucky to get away from Avoch-Dar and the demons with our *lives*, let alone the book."

"Perhaps if the situation had been handled by someone with greater knowledge, and a more just claim to the book—"

"Not that again! The someone is you, right?

When are you going to get it through your thick head that Leandor was the one spoken of in the prophecy? He was *destined* to seek the book!"

"That is how you and he choose to interpret it. But surely it makes more sense that mastery of the book should be in the hands of someone who serves the gods? Rather than…"

"Than what?"

"Rather than a man who is at base little more than a professional killer. And obviously an incompetent one at that. I mean, he not only lost the book to Avoch-Dar but also his arm. Then, as I understand it, he ran away. It seems to me—"

"What?" Once more her exasperation with the monk was swiftly turning to anger. "He lost his arm as a result of a foul magic spell! I'd like to have seen *you* do better in the circumstances!"

"Shani, I—"

"To brand him a common killer is a disgrace!" she ploughed on. "Leandor was the King's Champion, not some footpad stalking victims in dark alleys!"

"If you'd just let me—"

"And you're a hypocrite, Hadzor! You've taken lives yourself in the brief time I've known you!"

He was growing flushed. His temper too was rising. "That was for a justifiable reason! I would never offer violence to the innocent!"

"It's no different with Leandor! You make him sound like some kind of hired assassin, and that's not right at all!"

They had reached a division in the rough track they followed, with paths snaking off in different directions. The monk pulled up his horse. Shani did likewise.

"You accuse me of ignorance," he fumed, "but you seem unaware yourself of the peril we face! The coming of the sorcerer, the recovery of the book, the demons' return all point to a final conflict! Unless someone opposes this evil, Humanity's days are numbered!"

She tried to cool things by sounding reasonable. "Tell Leandor all this. If what you say is right, he has the authority to raise an army and—"

"What point is there in wasting time by going to him again? What more can he add? It's action that's needed, not talk!"

"Don't be a fool, Hadzor. There are easier ways to commit suicide than facing Avoch-Dar alone."

"If you and Leandor won't see sense, what choice do I have? I was a fool to waste my breath on either of you!"

"Stop for a moment and discuss this rationally. There has to be a better way."

"Will you come with me?"

"I … I *can't*. We must go back to—"

"End of discussion! If you won't accompany me to Vaynor, I'm quite capable of getting there by myself!"

He began reining his horse to the right-hand track.

Shani abandoned her attempt to talk some sense into him. "You ... *stubborn idiot*!" she raged.

He spurred his mount from her and along the south-east path.

"Go ahead and court death, see if I care!" she yelled.

He did not reply or even turn to look back.

Boiling with anger, she sat for a moment and watched him ride away.

Then she guided her horse on to the other trail and galloped in the direction of Allderhaven.

"This seems such a pointless exercise," Leandor complained, "in view of recent events."

"It is a very necessary task," Tycho insisted.

It was mid-morning in Allderhaven, and the snow-lined streets were beginning to fill with people. Some recognized the Champion and paused to stare; a few waved greetings.

"With a new threat from Avoch-Dar, surely my time could be better spent than by inspecting the building works?" he said.

"Making sure our defences are being properly restored *is* time well spent," the homunculus assured him. "It could prove vital should the sorcerer invade once more."

"Somehow I can't see him taking such a direct

approach again, bearing in mind what little good it did him on the previous occasions. I suspect a more devious scheme."

"You could well be right, Dalveen. But until we have some solid information about his intentions, what else can you do? Scour the countryside in search of him? *That* would hardly be a sensible use of your time."

"The obvious thing would be to head for his most likely hiding-place. Vaynor."

"What if that's exactly the assumption he wants you to make? Either to lay a trap for you or to attack the capital once you've gone? Even both?"

Leandor sighed. "I don't know what to do for the best, Tycho."

Had they not been so wrapped up in their conversation, they might have noticed they were being followed.

The figure dogging them took advantage of the hiding-places provided by the jumble of buildings in this run-down part of the city. Someone who despite his size skilfully concealed himself in the shadows and gloomy alleyways daylight did not penetrate.

"How is Bethan after last night's extraordinary events?" Tycho asked.

"Still shaken, but I think she'll be all right. Fortunately she inherited a good measure of the steel that stiffened her father's backbone."

"I have pondered a great deal on what we witnessed. Melva's words, and the King's, not to mention Karale's mysterious departure, have been much in my thoughts."

"And mine. Particularly Eldrick's remarks about these being the last days."

"That was certainly intriguing. However, my mind has been turning on the weapon Melva told you about; what it could be, and where it is."

"It would have to be a mighty weapon indeed to make much difference in a fight with Avoch-Dar and the demons."

"What I was wondering," Tycho said, "is whether the wizard also knows of this weapon's existence. Because if he does, no doubt he will try to reach it before you."

"That hadn't occurred to me," Leandor admitted. "But would its whereabouts be any clearer to him than to Melva?"

"With the demons' aid, perhaps it would."

"Well, it isn't something we can worry about at the moment." He looked around the area they had entered. It was quieter here, with hardly anyone else about. "Where to now?"

"An observation tower near the outer wall. That way." Tycho pointed to a narrow, downward-sloping lane. The tall buildings it ran between starved the thoroughfare of light.

Waiting until they entered, the bulky figure

trailed them.

At the cobbled lane's far end they came to the base of the tower. Scaffolding had been erected to about half its height. But there were no labourers to be seen.

"Work has stopped here because of a shortage of money," Tycho explained. "It's your decision whether it should start again."

"An observation point is vital to our defences. Order work resumed immediately and—"

"*Nightshade!*"

They spun around.

And faced an awesome sight.

He was at least a head and shoulders taller than Leandor, and as broad as two ordinary men. His solid frame rippled with muscles, and he was completely bald.

Notwithstanding the cold, an open, sleeveless jerkin made from animal furs was all that covered his bare chest. Below that he wore tight black breeches tucked into knee-length tan boots, with a wide leather belt secured by a gold buckle the size of a dinner plate.

He held a huge double-headed axe.

Leandor calmly returned his gaze. "I don't think I've had the pleasure of an introduction."

The man threw back his head and roared with laughter. "You're cool, Leandor, I'll give you that. My name is Soma Hobbe."

"What business do you have with me, Hobbe?"

"The business of death. And I expect to earn a healthy profit!"

"That would be very pleasant for you," Leandor told him evenly, "if it were possible."

"I'll show you how possible it is!"

"Before you try, perhaps you might tell me who places such a high value on my life."

"As I heard it, you and a woman called Vanya killed some leading members of the Brotherhood of Assassins and the Guild of Thieves. They can't afford to lose face like that. So they're offering a very, *very* large bounty to anybody who can bring them your heads."

"And you intend collecting?"

"I've already beaten two rivals to get here first. I'll collect."

"I see." He gave the axeman a relaxed smile. "Well, if you feel you must... But there's still time for you to walk away."

"You can't wriggle your way out of it, one-arm!" Hobbe snarled disdainfully. Then he looked down at Tycho and said, "If you don't want to get hurt, little freak, you'll stay out of this."

"As it happens, I was made in such a fashion that I am incapable of harming human life," the homunculus informed him. "Although at times such as this I find it an irksome restriction."

The bounty hunter boomed with laughter again.

"How lucky I am!" he mocked. "I was quaking in my boots at the thought of tangling with a dwarf ball of fluff." Instantly his mirth vanished and he barked, *"Out of my sight!"* A backhand swipe sent Tycho to the cobblestones.

Leandor glanced at his friend, then looked up at Hobbe, eyes hardening like flint. "So that's your way, is it? Picking on the defenceless rather than taking a chance with someone likely to hit back."

"And is it the great Nightshade's practice to *talk* people to death?" Hobbe growled. He raised the axe. "Do you yield?"

"I yield to no man."

"Then fill your hand, cur!"

Before he could reach for his sword, almost before he had time to think, Hobbe's weapon was swinging at his head.

Leandor flung himself aside. The axe struck the wall of the tower, dashing blue sparks from the masonry. He back-stepped a few paces as he drew his blade. And immediately had to dodge the scything axe again.

If Leandor thought his opponent was going to be a lumbering colossus, he was wrong. Hobbe's movements were astonishingly fast for a man of his size.

Forced to retreat by the relentless onslaught, Leandor had yet to strike an answering blow. It was all he could do to avoid the twin-headed axe's deadly bite. He was probably swifter than Hobbe, but the man was never still. Leandor couldn't see a way through his defences.

Leandor knew that in theory a fight between blade and axe usually gave the swordsman an advantage. A sword is lighter and easier to bring into play, and has the longer reach.

Hobbe's immense strength and surprising agility were disproving that theory.

A bold move was called for. When the next swing came at him, he stayed put for a split second longer than he should. Then instead of going back or to the side he dropped into a crouch. As the axe whistled overhead he slashed at Hobbe's legs. The sword tip raked above his left knee, laying open the flesh.

Hobbe bellowed with rage.

He directed the axe in a downward arc. It would have cleaved Leandor's back had he not dived out of reach. But that left him stretched full-length on the ground. And before he could get to his feet Hobbe had caught up.

The axe came down with tremendous force. Leandor rolled and barely evaded the stroke. Cobblestones shattered under the impact. Shards flew in all directions.

All he could do was keep rolling. Hobbe came after him, raining down blows, each narrowly missing the target. Tiny explosions of stone were thrown up where the axe pounded the lane's surface.

Battered by the cobbles, his face and body grazed, Leandor spun twice more then slammed into a wall.

It knocked the breath out of him. He was dazed and disoriented.

Hobbe appeared above him and drew back the axe for a lethal stroke.

CHAPTER 11

Leandor looked up at the figure towering above him. The great axe glinted in the watery sunshine.

Then some of the fug cleared from his head and he realized he was still clutching his sword.

He lashed upwards with it, hoping to catch his foe's unprotected mid-section. But the axe was already coming down, and the edge of his blade sliced across Hobbe's knuckles instead.

It was enough. The bounty hunter yelled. His intended blow's trajectory was altered and the axe gashed a lump out of the wall.

Scrambling clear, Leandor gained his feet, ran a few paces and turned.

Hobbe was there, no more than a blade's length in front of him. And his axe was already swinging.

Leandor moved rapidly to one side and avoided the full impact. But not fast enough to escape entirely. The axe sliced along the length of his arm. Its keen edge shredded his sleeve, gouging the skin beneath.

The sword flew from his hand and clattered on the cobbles.

He pulled back, blood streaming from the wound. Hobbe kept coming.

A storm of slashes from the axe forced Leandor to retreat further. Then something stopped him. He had backed into a central support of the tower's scaffolding.

Hobbe unleashed a great arcing slice. Leandor ducked. The axe embedded itself in the wooden upright.

As the bounty hunter struggled to free his weapon, Leandor got himself out of range. But Hobbe stood between him and his sword.

Then for the first time since the fight began, Leandor noticed Tycho. The homunculus couldn't get to the sword either without coming too close to Hobbe. He was standing on the other side of the lane, quite motionless, with an arm outstretched. Leandor guessed what he was trying to do.

The sword moved, just a fraction, across the cobbled surface.

A splintering sound drew his attention back to Hobbe. He had jerked loose the axe, hewing a chunk from the upright in the process. Now he turned to renew the attack.

Under Tycho's magical control, the sword slowly rose from the ground.

Unaware of this, his face murderous, Hobbe advanced. Leandor prepared to defend himself as best he could. He eyed the axe.

A silvery blur soared through the air to the bounty hunter's right.

He turned his head and exclaimed, "*What the—?*"

Leander reached out and snatched the flying sword's hilt.

Without pause he lunged at Hobbe, directing a series of offensive strokes at him. Still bewildered by the demonstration of Tycho's power of levitation, the axeman's response was sluggish.

But his confusion didn't last long. He began parrying the blows, and was soon near getting the upper hand again.

Leandor had assumed there was a limit to how long his opponent could go on expending so much energy. He was now starting to see Hobbe wasn't going to be easily worn out. There had to be a way of turning the tide.

Then he noticed something that gave him an idea.

Leandor feigned a retreat. For every swing of Hobbe's axe he went back a pace or two and edged left. A triumphant grin on the bounty hunter's face showed he swallowed the deception. If he grew overly confident, that could be helpful too.

Careful not to give himself away by looking behind him, Leandor continued to withdraw and circle. He kept up the pretence until they reached the scaffolding.

Now the plan depended on positioning himself in exactly the right place.

He allowed himself to be driven backwards into the rows of timber uprights. It was a dangerous strategy. As well as having to avoid the axe, he had to weave his way through the wooden obstructions.

Finally his back came into contact with the main support. He hoped the expression of fearful surprise he faked was convincing.

Hobbe's lips stretched in a victorious smirk, revealing yellow, broken teeth. He drew back the double-bladed axe and aimed a massive swing at his quarry's neck.

Leandor forced himself to remain absolutely still as the curved, razor sharp hunk of cold steel winged toward him.

At the last possible second he dropped like a dead weight.

The axe whistled over his head and clean through the already weakened timber upright. There was a series of loud, ominous cracking noises from above. Hobbe looked up, a stupefied expression on his face.

Leandor didn't stay to relish it. He ran.

As he dashed between the rows of lesser support poles he struck out at them with his sword. Left, right, left, with lightning rapidity he cleaved through all the uprights he passed. The whole structure creaked and groaned.

Then he was clear and running toward Tycho, yelling, *"Take cover!"*

He smacked into the homunculus and they hit the cobblestones.

Leandor looked back. Hobbe was blundering his way through the scaffolding. Pieces of wood and debris rained down all around him. A heavy coil of rope struck his shoulder. A plank slammed to earth beside him.

The bounty hunter raised his axe and bellowed.

A sound like thunder drowned him out.

And the entire construction collapsed.

Leandor and Tycho caught a glimpse of several tons of plunging timber and masonry. Then a thick cloud of white dust and bouncing stones swept towards them and they hid their faces.

The weighty crash and rumble gave way to silence.

They got up.

"Are you all right?" Leandor asked.

"Perfectly," Tycho replied. "More to the point, how are you?" He glanced at Leandor's ragged sleeve.

"Fine. I've had worse injuries. And thanks for your help with the sword." He slipped it into his scabbard.

Brushing dust from their clothes and fur, they approached the foot of the tower.

All there was to be seen of Soma Hobbe was his tan-booted legs, sticking out from the tangled mass.

"I think he found it a somewhat crushing experience," Leandor remarked dryly.

"I've never been able to understand how you humans can joke about such dangerous circumstances," the homunculus said, his face deadpan.

Leandor smiled. "It's one of the things that *makes* us human. No offence, Tycho."

"None taken. Indeed I hope that in due course I may develop what you call a sense of humour myself." He surveyed the mountain of clutter. "This is going to be expensive to put right. And it's a cost we can ill afford."

"It was almost worth it."

Tycho was mystified. "All this destruction worthwhile? How so?"

"Because it reminded me of how *real* combat

feels. I've spent too long hacking at targets and fighting mock duels in training. There's nothing like facing someone determined to kill you. It … wakes you up."

"Your insistence on dicing with death is something else I'll never understand about humans," Tycho sighed. "But one thing this confrontation proves is that the King's shade was right in saying you should expect to meet powerful enemies."

"Yes. And despite what I just said, I could do without the complication. It's bad enough having to anticipate Avoch-Dar's next move."

"I shall arrange to have this mess cleared. And you should have that wound attended to, no matter how slight you claim it is."

"As soon as we get to the palace."

Drawn by the sounds of uproar, people were leaning out of windows, trying to see what was going on. Others appeared further along the lane, but kept their distance.

Leandor and Tycho began moving off. "We must also address the problem of the other two bounty hunters Hobbe mentioned," the homunculus stated. "And for all we know there could be more."

"I'll stay alert."

"It isn't just you, Dalveen. Remember that Hobbe told us there is a price on Shani's head as well."

Leandor frowned. "Damn, you're right."

"And she may well not be aware of the fact. I know she's perfectly capable of looking after herself, but nevertheless she should be warned."

"I agree. What do you suggest?"

"I would like to seek her out myself. My work here can be handled quite adequately by deputies while I'm away."

"But why you?"

"First, I have the obvious advantage of knowing Shani. Second, as a friend, I would hope to be able to persuade her to return to Allderhaven. I feel her presence could be most valuable in light of the new threat from Avoch-Dar. If you have no objections, that is?"

Leandor thought about it for a second. "None," he decided. "I would welcome her return. However it's best if we set a time limit on your search. And I don't want you venturing out unaccompanied; I'll select a small detail of fighting men for your protection."

"Thank you, Dalveen."

"When will you set off?"

"As soon as possible. Indeed, I am quite looking forward to it. Who knows? Perhaps I am developing a small urge for adventure myself."

"We'll make a human of you yet," Leandor grinned.

CHAPTER 12

It was time to feed the Book of Shadows again.
The demons had gathered in the Great Hall to witness the rite.

Avoch-Dar still marvelled at how no two of the hellish horde seemed to look alike. He suspected, but did not know for sure, that they could change their appearance at will. So when he saw them all together he tended not to perceive them as individuals. Rather there was a general impression of leathery skin, scales, feathers, slimy hides and fur. Of claws, fangs, suckers and tentacles; multiple sets of eyes, eyes on stalks, slitty eyes of remarkable colours, and no eyes at all. And other bodily parts for which names did not exist.

The Sygazon were amazingly varied in their loath-someness.

He thought them quite delightful.

Lord Berith acted as their spokesman – if any title including "man" could be applied to such a creature – but did not seem to be their leader. It appeared they had none, preferring to act collectively.

Berith had never changed appearance during Avoch-Dar's time with the demons. Perhaps this was a way of making itself identifiable and easier to deal with. Or there might have been another reason the sorcerer couldn't even guess at. There was so much to learn about them.

The wizard and the demon lord stood beside the altar.

"How many today?" Berith hissed.

"Two," Avoch-Dar said. "A couple of brigands found by a patrol on Pandemonium's outskirts."

"Hardly quality material."

"At the moment we have to make do with what we can get. As our dominion spreads we will have access to sacrifices of a higher standard. As many as the book could possibly need."

A group of guards ushered in the bound prisoners. They were sorry looking specimens: bedraggled, exhausted, the worse for a night in the palace's dreadful dungeons.

What they could see of the demons, skulking in the semi-darkness at the edge of the hall, turned their apprehension to fear.

At sight of Berith it gave way to open terror.

They struggled against their bonds, cursed and

pleaded. The guards used their spears to prod them in the direction of the altar.

The Book of Shadows lay open, surrounded by a shimmering blue haze.

The captives were forced to their knees before it.

A rhythmic chant, unearthly and inhuman, rose from the assembled Sygazon. The prisoners exchanged glances part horrified, part bewildered.

An intense throbbing permeated the luminescence about the book. It passed through all tones of blue, from indigo to sapphire, azure to turquoise.

Twin forks of radiance like bolts of lightning snaked out, instantly connecting with the crown of the men's heads.

They screamed.

For several seconds the prisoners writhed. Their bodies visibly shrank.

Then the dazzling bolts flickered and died.

Two smouldering husks were left, sucked dry and collapsed in on themselves. An odour of charred flesh hung in the air.

Avoch-Dar snapped his fingers. Guards moved forward and began dragging away the remains.

*"The book seems insatiable since it was reawakened,"
Berith observed. "It must be kept supplied with life essences."*

"I'll see to it," the wizard promised. "But I confess I am still surprised that the tome requires sacrifices at all."

"That is one of the least surprising of its many qualities," the demon replied. "As with all life-forms it must replenish itself by consuming food. It lay undiscovered in Zenobia for a span of time most humans would find unimaginable, and was starved of vital energies. It is making up for that now."

"Will it reach a point where its hunger is satisfied?"

"It has never been known to."

Avoch-Dar dwelt upon the implications of that fact. If there was no limit to the life essences the book devoured it must grow in strength, which was another way of saying its magical power would become yet greater. That made it an even more desirable prize.

Berith's manifold eyes glinted slyly. "How goes the plot against Nightshade?"

The question brought the wizard out of his reverie. "All arrangements have been made. I strike soon. Very soon."

"Whatever you may think of him, Nightshade is an extremely dangerous opponent, perhaps more dangerous than he realizes himself," the demon remarked mysteriously. "And because of this we judge you ready for a portion of the additional power you crave to assist your scheme."

Avoch-Dar's lips stretched in a smile of triumphant satisfaction.

The glowing light given off by the book turned deep crimson.

*   *   *

Bethan watched as one of her ladies-in-waiting dressed Leandor's wound.

"Does it trouble you much?" she asked anxiously.

"No," he replied, "it really isn't serious."

"It could have been, given what you've told me about the savagery of your attacker."

"But it wasn't, Bethan. And the occasional injury is the lot of a fighting man. It comes with the profession."

"A profession I could sometimes wish you didn't follow," she said moodily.

The lady-in-waiting finished applying the dressing. Leandor smiled his thanks and Bethan dismissed her.

As she curtsied and left, Dalveen turned to Tycho. "Have you made ready for your journey?"

"Yes, and I have briefed my deputies on what needs to be done while I'm away."

"Where do you intend searching?"

"The most recent sightings of Shani our agents reported placed her in the region of the northern forests. I'll begin there."

"All right. But as I said, we'll set a limit on your absence. A week should be enough. Agreed?"

"I'm sure that will be adequate."

"I want you taking no unnecessary risks, hear? That part of the country has several pockets of lawlessness. Bearsden, for example. Which incidentally I intend cleaning out as soon as our present … difficulties are settled. Meantime, watch your back."

"I'll be careful."

"I've picked a sergeant and two troopers to go with you. They're good men, and should be able to handle any problems you might meet."

"Thank you, Dalveen." The homunculus got up. "If that's all, I would like to take advantage of the remaining light and be on my way."

Leandor extended his bandaged arm. He and Tycho clasped each other's wrists, warrior fashion. "Fare thee well, my friend. And good fortune."

Bethan leaned over and planted a kiss on Tycho's hairy cheek. "Gods be with you."

When he had taken his leave, she said, "Do you consider Shani's presence here so important that Tycho can be spared for a whole week? Not to mention the peril he may face."

"The main reason for his going is to warn her about the other bounty hunters. If he can also persuade her to accompany him back here, that's a bonus. And yes, I think her presence important. She fights as well as any warrior I've ever known and keeps a cool head in a crisis."

"I see," the Princess responded frostily.

Before he could reply there was a rap at the door.

"Enter!" Bethan snapped.

Quixwood came in. He had three members of

the Palace Guard in tow. They remained standing just inside the entrance.

"Is this a convenient time, Dalveen?"

Leandor glanced at Bethan. She made no protest. "Certainly, Golcar. What can I do for you?"

"Keep your temper in check."

Leandor was puzzled. "Why shouldn't I?"

"Because you're likely to take offence at what I'm about to suggest."

"Explain yourself and we'll see."

Quixwood pointed to the trio of guardsmen. "These officers are known to you, and you're familiar with their excellent service records."

"Yes. What of it?"

"I want you to agree to them acting as your bodyguard."

"As my…? *Come on*, Golcar."

"Hear me out. What with at least two bounty hunters stalking you, and who knows what new perils in store from Avoch-Dar, it makes sense."

"But I've never—"

"You've never felt in need of bodyguards before, I know. And it will probably hurt your pride to admit you might need them now."

"I think I can handle any danger I'm likely to meet."

"No one doubts it, lad. But it's foolish for someone in your position to take chances. The fact is you're too valuable to lose."

"Did you know about this, Bethan?" Leandor asked.

"Golcar mentioned it to me earlier. I think it's a good idea. And if you won't do it for yourself, think about the rest of us. Think about *me*."

"They'll just be there to back you up," Quixwood added. "You must see the value in having some extra swords around."

Leandor looked at the five expectant faces, and after a moment's consideration reluctantly said, "All right. But just for the time being! I don't want this turning into a permanent arrangement. It's only for as long as it takes to sort things out."

"That's my boy," a delighted Quixwood told him.

"Accept it with good grace, Dalveen," Bethan advised him.

"That may be asking just a little *too* much," he said, eyeing the guards. "Now if you'll excuse me, I'm in need of solitude. I have some thinking to do."

He bade them farewell and made for the door. The trio of guardsmen stiffened to attention.

"Come on, then," he sighed.

They fell in behind him.

He led them to Torpoint's farthest tower, and up the winding staircase to what was once Avoch-Dar's sanctuary. Assuring them he would be perfectly safe, he ordered the men to wait outside.

Once in the chamber, Leandor pulled over a chair and sat in front of the dead crystal.

He appreciated the quiet of this place. It would help him work out what his next move should be.

He must have fallen asleep.

There was no way of knowing how much time had passed. And something had woken him. His first thought, as he blinked the slumber from his eyes, was of the crystal. But it remained dead.

Then he was aware of a movement in the chamber's dimmest corner. He leapt up, drawing his sword. "Who's there?" he demanded. "Show yourself!"

A figure stepped out of the gloom.

"Did I wake you, Nightshade?" Avoch-Dar enquired sarcastically.

Leandor doubted his senses for a moment. "*You?* Here? You must be mad to put yourself in range of my blade."

The sorcerer came a step closer. Fearful he would cast a spell, Leandor lunged forward and slashed at him. His sword passed through the wizard's body, meeting no more resistance than it would from empty air.

Avoch-Dar laughed. "Impressive, isn't it?" he gloated. "A new ability I simply couldn't wait to show you. Just a small demonstration of the powers my demon friends have conferred upon me."

Leandor was gathering his wits, and would be damned rather than let the man see how shaken he was. "It seems there's a price attached to the gifts the demons bestow," he retorted. "You look more repulsive every time I see you. Exposing yourself to their influence is corrupting your flesh, sorcerer!"

"You suppose I care? I would gladly rot to my bones in exchange for what they can give me!"

"I will seek you out," Leandor promised. "I will track you to whatever stinking lair you inhabit and separate your foul head from its body." He trusted his instinct and threw in a wild guess. "And I warrant the sewer you inhabit is Vaynor."

"You think me back in Vaynor? Well, I won't deny it. In any event you won't live long enough to use the knowledge. And when I've done with you, my wrath will turn against your bride-to-be, and everyone else you hold dear."

"So you're here to bluster, and to issue more empty threats. How very predictable."

"My threats are never empty, Leandor. But on this occasion I merely wish to bid you a final farewell."

"Not final, carrion crow. Our goodbyes will come when my blade meets your heart."

"We shall see. Oh, how silly of me. There is one more thing." He raised his hands. "I'm going to take something back. In a way."

Vivid memories flooded into Leandor's mind. He recalled standing on the field of battle facing the sorcerer. Avoch-Dar had raised his hands then, too, and cast a spell that deprived Leandor of his arm.

A cold shiver caressed his spine. He braced himself.

The wizard turned and stretched out his arms, pointing them at the crystal. He made a rapid series of complicated gestures.

A searing bolt of pure energy erupted from his fingertips.

The gem exploded with a deafening blast.

Leandor threw up his arm to cover his face as thousands of tiny fragments flew out in all directions. Scores of shards peppered him.

When he uncovered his face, Avoch-Dar was rocking with scornful laughter. His expression was the most depraved thing Leandor had ever seen.

Then the sorcerer weaved another conjuration with his hands and vanished.

Air rushed in to fill the space he had occupied.

With a crash the door flew open. The three bodyguards thundered into the room, swords drawn, crunching over the scattered remnants of the crystal. They gazed at the mess.

"Are you all right, sir?" one of them asked.

Leandor looked down at himself. None of the

gem's glassy fragments had cut him, or even penetrated his clothing.

He regarded the ashen faces of his guardians.

"I'm ... all right," he told them. "All right."

But that wasn't the way he felt.

CHAPTER 13

Shani didn't exactly hunger for company, but after three days of solitude she welcomed seeing another face. And one of her horse's shoes needed replacing.

The settlement she came across was small, and if it had a name she saw no sign proclaiming it. But as this makeshift collection of ramshackle dwellings stood on the shores of a river flowing from the mountains, she guessed the inhabitants were gold-panners.

She took a chance on them being friendly and rode in.

Tracks through the frozen mud served as streets. They were practically deserted, perhaps because most of the citizens were out prospecting. Such people as were about paid her little attention.

One of the more substantial buildings on what passed for the main avenue proved to be a blacksmith's. The smithy was a big, genial man, and he promised to have the horse shod in an hour. He also directed her to the town's only inn. It turned out to be more welcoming than the last one she'd visited.

There were few customers, but only one topic of conversation: the King's death.

The news saddened her, and she regretted having not been in Allderhaven to lend Dalveen and Bethan her support. She was all the more determined to get there without further delay, and hurried to finish her meal.

In melancholy mood she trudged back to the blacksmith's.

It was deserted. A fire was still burning in the forge so she assumed the smithy would soon return. Her horse was stabled in the back of the building. Its shoe had been changed. Not wanting to leave without paying, she sat on the anvil and waited.

And waited.

Shani thought it odd that the place should be unattended for so long. But mostly she grew impatient to continue her journey. Finally she decided to leave the money where the smithy would find it. An oak table set to one side seemed the logical place. She went over to it, digging coins from her pocket.

Then she noticed something partially hidden by a pile of hay. Curious, she knelt to investigate, brushing the fodder aside with her hands.

She found the blacksmith's body.

There was a thin red line of broken skin round his neck, indicating strangulation with something like a garrotte. The lack of other injuries pointed to him not having had time to put up a fight. It would have taken skill and strength to better a man of his size. The hallmarks of a professional killer.

Shani was wondering what to do when she realized she wasn't alone. She looked up.

A woman was walking towards her from the stabling pens at the rear of the building. Her appearance was striking.

Young, although probably a couple of years older than Shani, she was tall and athletically built. Long, flame-red hair cascaded over her shoulders.

She was clad entirely in black: skin-tight leather breeches and top, thigh-length suede riding boots. The sleeves and upper fronts of her jacket, and sides of her boots, were decorated with silver studs. There was a leather choker around her throat, prickling with tiny spikes, and she wore spiked wristbands above gauntlets.

A snub-bladed sword hung in a scabbard at her

waist. She held a coiled whip.

"We meet at last, Shani Vanya," she said. Her expression was hard and cold, her lips cruel.

Shani wondered why just about everybody she met recently seemed to know her. "Who the hell are *you*?"

"My name's Jocasta Marrell. Don't bother learning it, you won't be around long enough."

Shani ignored the threat and indicated the dead blacksmith. "Your work?"

"I thought we could do with a little privacy. Now are you going to get up and face me or do you prefer to die kneeling down?"

"Well, you talk a good fight. If I were looking for one. What exactly have I done to upset you?"

"Idle chit-chat's so boring don't you think?" With a deft wrist movement she uncoiled the whip. "So rather than waste breath I'll just kill you and get it over with, shall I?"

"I'd like to see you try!" Shani exclaimed, leaping to her feet.

Instantly the woman's whip lashed Shani's left arm. The stinging pain made her gasp and quickly back off.

Marrell cracked the whip at her again. Shani narrowly dodged it, and the next lash, which came perilously close to her face.

The suddenness and ferocity of the attack had taken her by surprise. But she had to do better than a blundering retreat. She needed to seize the initiative.

Side-stepping to avoid another lashing, she pulled out a knife and flung it.

The throw wasn't bad, though unconsidered, and should have ended in her opponent's chest. But it was destined not to.

Swift as lightning, Marrell snapped the whip outwards and struck the flying blade. It deflected and spun away harmlessly.

Shani was astonished. And despite her irritation and anger she felt a flash of admiration for the woman's skill.

"Is that the best you can do, Vanya?" Marrell taunted. "Your reputation's overrated!"

Another crack of the whip. Another miss too close for comfort.

Shani plucked a second knife. She lobbed it directly at Marrell's head.

The woman moved fast enough to avoid a hit. Just. It skimmed over her shoulder and smacked into the wooden wall behind her. Her eyes flared with hatred and she immediately retaliated.

A slender blur, the whip slashed low, its tip catching Shani above the right knee. It felt like a hot poker had been plunged into her.

"Hell's teeth!" she cried.

Her temper was near boiling point. No way was she going to let this female best her. She grasped a third blade and tossed it with all the force she could muster.

Marrell was drawing the whip back to crack again, and the swiftness of the throw took her off guard. She tumbled to the side, but couldn't evade the knife. It skimmed through the top of her gloved hand, ripping it open.

"Damnation!" she yelled.

Shani had already drawn a further blade. But she realized a change of strategy was called for. They circled warily, viewing each other with grudging respect.

It seemed to Shani they were heading for a stand-off unless she did something bold. She had to get past the whip and take the fight in close.

Marrell suddenly began lashing out with fresh vigour. Shani avoided the first couple of strokes then made up her mind to act. It was going to hurt like blazes but she couldn't see any other way of doing it.

She let the next whipcrack come straight at her. It would have struck squarely at her neck, except at the last moment she brought up her free hand. The whip wrapped it, stinging like a burning ember. She quickly clenched her fist, looped the strap around her wrist and pulled with all her might.

Morrell gave a surprised, rather unladylike grunt and flew forward. Shani met her with the knuckles of her other fist, delivering a sharp blow to the chin. Morrell went down, letting go of her end of the whip. Shani threw it clear and levelled the knife.

Her foe recovered right away, scrambling to her feet and snatching the sword from its scabbard. It was a short-bladed weapon, designed for close combat. She rushed in, slashing wildly.

Sword and knife met with a steely clash. And it was all Shani could do to hang on to her modest blade in face of the sword's larger strokes. She tried to avoid contact; feigning, parrying and slashing, ever seeking a path through her opponent's defences.

They fought to the open doors and spilled out into the street. Neither gave the other quarter, nor expected it.

Then an unlucky stroke dashed the knife from Shani's hand.

Marrell pressed the advantage, slicing continuously, harrying Shani so thoroughly that she couldn't reach for another blade for fear of being run through. Marrell lunged forward, aiming for the heart. Shani spun and grabbed her wrist, simultaneously kicking out at her legs.

They collapsed in a struggling heap. The sword was lost.

Shani kept her grip on Marrell's wrist, clasping a handful of the woman's hair with her other hand. She pulled hard, forcing back her head.

Marrell tried the same thing, but Shani's hair was cut too short for it to work.

They rolled in the snowy mud, kicking and punching.

"Shani!"

The voice was distant, and for a moment she thought she'd imagined it. Then it came again.

She glanced along the street and saw four riders in the distance, galloping their way. Marrell saw them too, and took advantage of the distraction. She landed two enormous whacks to the side of Shani's face, breaking her hold, then leapt to her feet and ran.

Dazed, Shani got to her knees. She glimpsed Marrell, sword in hand, just inside the blacksmith's. She picked up the whip and disappeared into the building's dark interior.

The horsemen arrived. Three wore uniforms Shani recognized. The fourth had on grey robes and a cowl that covered most of his face.

At that moment Marrell thundered out of the blacksmith's on her own steed and raced in the opposite direction. Two of the riders peeled off and gave chase.

The robed horseman dismounted and threw back his hood.

"Tycho!" she gasped.

"Are you all right?" he asked anxiously, taking her arm.

"Never better," she told him, smiling through the pain. "And the more so for seeing you, old friend!" She threw her arms around him.

The homunculus's embarrassment was so obvious she had to laugh.

"Are you sure you sustained no wounds?" he said.

"Nothing too serious. Though that she-cat was good. *Very* good. But don't ask me who the hell she was."

"I think I might know, Shani."

"You do? And what the hell are you *doing* here, anyway?"

"Looking for you."

"That seems to be a popular sport at the moment."

"Pardon?"

"Don't worry, I'll explain later."

The two riders returned at a clip and pulled up beside them. "Sorry, sir," one of them apologized. "She got a head start on us and there's no sign of her. Do you want us to search farther afield?"

Tycho looked at Shani. "Don't bother," she said.

"No, leave it for now," he told the escort. "We'll rest here for a while."

"She killed the blacksmith," Shani explained. "His body's in there. It might be better to get away before people start asking awkward questions."

"As strangers we're bound to be blamed," Tycho

agreed, "and my appearance would hardly aid our defence. Are you fit enough to ride?"

She nodded.

"Then I suggest we talk on the road."

"The road to Allderhaven?"

"Yes. Unless—"

"That's where I was heading."

"Good. Your presence will be most useful, I'm sure."

"Something big's brewing, isn't it, Tycho?"

"I believe so. There is much to tell you."

"That's just what I was about to say."

She limped off to fetch her horse.

Avoch-Dar and Berith stood together, gazing down into the remote viewing pool.

The other demons were present. But as usual they stayed in the ill-lit nooks and corners, fulfilling their cryptic, incomprehensible purposes.

Berith was not best pleased with the sorcerer.

"Why do you persist in showing yourself to Night-shade?" the demon wheezed. "Do you intend doing no more than mocking him from afar?"

"I intend obliterating him! As you are about to see. I taunt him in advance because it gives me pleasure."

"That is a very ... human thing to do. Your progress through the secret teachings will see an end to such petty emotions. You will cast off your humanity and be better for it."

"I could easily have killed Leandor when I appeared before him at Torpoint, you know," Avoch-Dar complained bitterly. "Had it not been impossible for me to do anything other than destroy the crystal."

"As I explained, to both physically project yourself to another location and harm life is a complicated magical procedure. You are not yet ready to attempt that without risking your own life. Until you are, you must work through others."

"Why can't you use your magic to strike down Leandor yourself? Surely that would be a simple enough task for the Sygazon?"

"We have our reasons." There was something about Berith's tone that forbade further argument. "Now proceed."

Avoch-Dar bit back his irritation. He had to remember that the power he lusted after required patience. Leaning forward, he conjured the necessary spell.

The green fluid bubbled and churned.

Then stilled as an image formed.

It showed Leandor in a courtyard at Torpoint. His trio of bodyguards could be seen in the background.

Grinning maniacally, the sorcerer set to work.

Leandor found one small benefit in having three Royal Guardsmen trailing him everywhere. He never had to look far for a sparring partner.

As he was still a little stiff from his fight with Hobbe, and knew from experience that combat practice was a good way of limbering up, he decided on an hour's swordplay.

He chose one of the smaller courtyards. Everyone was busy with duties elsewhere and it was deserted.

Each of the guards would take their turn in crossing swords with him. A coin was tossed to determine who went first and the winner stepped forward. His comrades settled on a bench to watch.

Leandor and his opponent drew their blades and squared off.

The duel started fairly gently. They exchanged standard moves, employed classic gambits, parried each other's thrusts. After a few minutes, Leandor was wishing his partner would put a bit more fire into it.

Almost immediately, the man obliged. His offensive carried more force, the arc of his swings grew wider. He started directing blows at vulnerable areas. Blows which had they connected would have done real damage.

Leandor was having to work harder and harder to fend off the attack. It began to dawn on him that something was wrong. The mild, almost polite honing of skills was starting to resemble a real fight. He wondered what lay behind the man's increasing ferocity.

Judging it time to call a halt, he stepped back and lowered his sword. His opponent ignored the gesture and swung at his head, forcing Leandor to duck.

"That's enough," he said.

The guardsman continued to press him, slashing wildly and trying to break through his defences.

"Hold!" Leandor ordered. "Hold, I say!"

The man took no notice.

Then Leandor noticed the look on his face. It was set in a kind of determined fury. And his eyes were … *wrong*. There was a trancelike quality about them, a cold, unfocused deadness.

Like the eyes of a corpse.

The pretence had vanished. This officer was a companion in arms, someone Leandor knew and had fought with. Now the man was trying to kill him.

Leandor was aware of movement at the bench. He glanced over. The other two bodyguards were on their feet, swords drawn. They were moving in.

And their eyes were dead, too.

CHAPTER 14

The sergeant rode ahead of Shani and Tycho, the pair of troopers brought up the rear.

"So Dalveen killed this Hobbe character, but you think Jocasta Marrell is one of the two remaining bounty hunters?" Shani said.

"It seems logical," Tycho replied. "Unless you have made other enemies recently you haven't mentioned."

"Oh, one or two. You know me!" She laughed. "But I'd never set eyes on her before. Do you know the identity of the third?"

"I'm afraid not."

Her expression became sombre. "Tell me, how are Dalveen and Bethan taking the King's death? And Golcar? He must be devastated."

"We are all very saddened, as you would expect. But there is much more afoot than even that, Shani."

He told her about the appearance of the King and Melva as apparitions. And the far less welcome visitation from Avoch-Dar, by way of his crystal.

"So he *is* back!" Shani exclaimed.

"Perhaps. Assuming he wasn't communicating with us from the demons' dimension."

"It looks like Hadzor was right."

"I know that name."

"How so?"

The homunculus related the story Leandor had told him about his meeting with Hadzor. In turn, Shani was able to add a few more facts.

"Have you ever heard of the Brotherhood of the Inner Light?" she asked.

"Vaguely. A long extinct holy order, is it not?"

"That's what I thought. But this Hadzor claimed they're still going and that he's a member."

"So he's a monk. How did you come to meet him?"

"Under rather ... vivid circumstances. I'll tell you about it later. The point is that he's apparently a student of the demon race and says he can read their language."

"Despite his self-deception, a man with such knowledge of the demons could be useful."

"I told him that. And we were on our way back

to Allderhaven together. Unfortunately he turned out to be one of the most stubborn cusses I've ever met and insisted on riding to Vaynor alone. He's convinced Avoch-Dar's returned there."

"His obsession must run deep indeed to do something that insane."

"Yes. A brave man, but a fool. If he's reached Vaynor yet he's probably already dead."

"Or suffering a worse fate if the sorcerer discovers he's a holy man. Avoch-Dar was never fond of servants of the gods." He looked up to check the sun's position in the sky. "Shani, I'd like to suggest that we push on with as few breaks for rest as possible. We should get back to Allderhaven with all speed."

"That's fine by me. The sooner I see Dalveen the better I'll feel. I've missed him."

"I would venture to say he feels the same way." He quickly added, "And Bethan too, of course."

"Of course." Her response was a mite stilted. Brightening, she asked, "What's he been up to?"

"Supervising the rebuilding work after Avoch-Dar's invasion mostly. He still pushes himself as hard as ever. But the Princess, Golcar and I have urged him to take it a little easier of late."

"Good. He deserves a rest after all he's been through." She pulled her jerkin tighter against the cold. "I could almost envy him; sitting in that warm palace, relaxing in luxury."

*   *   *

Leandor was fighting for his life.

The irony was that the men intent on his death had been assigned to protect him.

They were obviously under an enchantment, and he could guess who was behind it. But the fact that they were in some kind of trance state hadn't slowed their reflexes. Nor were they ordinary adversaries. As members of the Palace Guard, they were elite fighters. He had even supervised some of their training.

Because they were acting against their will, Leandor felt inhibited. He was holding back, reluctant to deal blows that could prove fatal.

But if he restrained himself much longer he was finished.

The first man who engaged him was still his main opponent. The other two sniped from the edges, striking at Leandor when the opportunity arose. He had to down them quickly, and preferably without killing them.

He ducked from the path of a wild swing, sidestepped and parried. A blade came in from the left. His sword flashed out and knocked it away. A jab from the right was deflected.

The man in front left himself open. It was a chance to see if pain would break the hex. Leandor slashed at his arm, instantly drawing blood. The man faltered for just a second before renewing his attack.

A swift flip of Leandor's blade to the right nicked the second man's cheek. There was no more than a fleeting reaction from him either.

It seemed that lightly wounding them wasn't enough.

He tried a different tack with the man to his left. Swinging at his sword with force, he aimed for the point where blade met hilt. The intention was to knock the weapon from his grasp. But the man's hold was unbreakable.

Leandor was near the stage where self-preservation was all that mattered. He was going to have to make his responses that much harder.

Then it occurred to him that if he couldn't shatter the men's trances, perhaps he might make them incapable of fighting.

A volley of blows came from left and right. His swift responses batted them away. The man facing him lunged forward, targeting his chest. Leandor swept the blade to one side.

Then set his plan in motion.

He retreated swiftly, dropped into a crouch and lashed at the man on his left. His swipe had all his strength behind it, and bit fiercely below both knees. The man staggered and went down. Leandor turned away, leaving him struggling feebly to stand.

The others closed in. Leandor drove one back. With the second he tried the same tactic, directing blows at the man's legs. But he had learned from his comrade's fate and was careful to keep out of range.

During the ensuing flurry of steel on steel, Leandor noticed a door opening at the far end of the courtyard.

Golcar Quixwood appeared. He stopped dead in his tracks and cried, *"Dalveen!"*

One of the guardsmen backed away from the fight and ran in his direction.

"Defend yourself, Golcar!" Leandor yelled.

The older man had enough presence of mind to draw his sword, just speedily enough to block his attacker's first swinging blow. Leandor heard Quixwood shouting the officer's name, trying to reason with him. It made no difference. A furious bout of fencing erupted.

Leandor was fearful for his adoptive father. Golcar had many years experience in swordplay, but his age was bound to tell on him in the end.

At least the distraction had left Leandor with only one opponent. He determined to deal with him quickly. And if that meant killing him, so be it. He slashed savagely at the man, pressing in without let, using every trick he knew to down him.

A stroke to the guardsman's upper chest should have finished it. But he managed to pull back at the last second. The tip of Leandor's blade raked through his shirt, ripping the fabric apart.

It cut through something else the man wore

beneath. A silver chain holding a medallion of some sort. The severed chain and the emblem it bore flew to the ground.

A kind of spasm ran through the man's body. He shook his head, blinking, and raised his free hand to his brow. His eyes had lost their deadness. Amazed, he gaped at Leandor, then down at the sword he held.

He dropped it like someone who found himself clutching a red hot poker.

Leandor stayed his next blow, a killing strike destined for his opponent's heart. He glanced at the discarded medallion. When he saw what it was, realization came.

"I … I don't… What…?" the man stammered, his face a picture of confusion.

"Get a hold on yourself," Leandor said. "It's all right."

A clash of swords from the courtyard's opposite end reminded him of Golcar. And the man felled earlier was still trying to rise and rejoin the battle.

"Get a grip!" Leandor barked at the dazed guardsman. He pointed to the man on the ground. "He's wearing a medallion around his neck. Get it off him. And watch for his sword!"

"Medallion…?"

"Yes. And do it *now!*"

Trusting that he had been understood, Leandor rushed off to aid Quixwood.

He arrived just in time. Golcar was flagging, and dangerously close to succumbing to one of the younger man's rain of blows.

Leandor now knew it wasn't necessary to kill Quixwood's opponent. Providing he was right in assuming he also wore a medallion. But trying to overpower rather than slay him made the situation even more perilous.

After a second's hesitation he resheathed his sword and approached the man from behind. What he had to do was no easy task for someone with only one arm. Speed was the key. Fortunately Quixwood, aware of Dalveen's stealthy advance, helped by keeping his foe occupied.

Leandor dived. He hit the man's back with enough force to send him sprawling forward. At the same time his hand snaked around his neck and plunged into his open shirt. His fingers touched a chain. He grasped it and pulled, snapping the links. The man stopped struggling and slumped.

Breathing hard, Leandor looked over to the others. The man with wounded legs was sitting with his head in his hands. His companion knelt beside him, studying something he held in his hand.

"Traitors!" Quixwood raged.

"No," Leandor panted. "Not traitors but directed by a magic spell. Look." He passed the medallion up to him.

It was a black pentagram.

"Avoch-Dar?" Quixwood said.

"Had to be. Each of these men wore one, and I'll wager the sorcerer controlled their minds by way of them. They're loyal officers, they shouldn't be blamed."

Quixwood stared at the medallion in his palm. "I'll be damned," he whispered.

"We all will if something isn't done." Leandor smiled weakly. "And if you don't mind, Golcar, I think I'll manage without bodyguards in future."

"Aye, lad. But how do we deal with the wizard, that's the question. If he can perform this kind of trick he's going to be more dangerous than ever."

"I've had enough of caution," Leandor declared, getting to his feet. "Now we take the war to the sorcerer!"

CҺAPTER 15

It was a mystery how Leandor's bodyguards came to be wearing the pentagram medallions. The men themselves had no recollection of being given them.

Quixwood's theory was that agents of Avoch-Dar had penetrated the barracks and slipped them about the guardsmen's necks as they slept, perhaps having first drugged their evening wine. When they awoke, they were under the sorcerer's control.

Leandor thought it as good an explanation as any. And he was thankful that his own sleeping quarters were too well protected to be entered. Had they not been, the wizard's minions would no doubt have attempted to deal with him in a more direct fashion.

Quixwood ordered a thorough tightening-up of security. Everyone in Torpoint, from the highest to the lowest, was searched to make sure they did not wear a medallion. Captains of the City Watch were told that should a citizen be discovered in possession of such a medallion they must be approached with caution, and were subject to immediate arrest. While this was going on, Leandor began preparing for his expedition.

But the following day was special, and plans for the journey were put aside.

It was the day chosen for Princess Bethan's coronation.

In consideration of the security situation it was decided to scale down the event and keep ceremonial trappings to a minimum. It was also Bethan's wish that no excessive fuss be made.

Despite decrees to this effect, it was still a national holiday and Allderhaven filled with revellers and parades, although on a more modest scale than in previous times.

All the guests and their retinues, even heads of neighbouring states, were searched for medallions. This brought protests from some, and the diplomats had their work cut out smoothing things over.

The climax came in mid-afternoon when Bethan walked up the rose petal strewn aisle in

Allderhaven's main temple. There, before the flower bedecked altar, the High Priest reverently placed the glittering crown on her head.

All hailed Queen Bethan of Delgarvo.

Much later, having fulfilled each ritual the day demanded, and spoken to everyone she had to thank, the new monarch retired to her private quarters.

Leandor followed her there, and with the sound of festivities ringing out in the streets below, pledged his own allegiance.

When he rose from kissing her hand, she said, "It may be rather un-queen like, but I can't wait to take this off." She removed the crown and carefully laid it on a table. "And if I don't sit down, I'll drop."

She settled on a couch and patted the adjacent space, indicating he should join her. He smiled and sank down on the cushions.

"How do you feel?" he asked.

"I feel as though I've committed myself to something ... awesome. I'm just beginning to get a sense of the responsibilities that go with being a queen. And it's a little frightening, Dalveen."

"I'm sure you'll handle it as well as everything you were called upon to do today."

"Truly?"

"I wouldn't lie to you, Bethan."

She grew more serious. "Then you'll tell me

honestly how dangerous this mission is you're embarking on."

"In truth, I don't know. But our past dealings with the sorcerer hardly bode well. And now he has the demons with him. I can't pretend it will be pleasant, or easy."

"And you are determined to set out tomorrow?"

"We leave for Vaynor at dawn."

"Can I not dissuade you? No, I can see from your face that I can't. Of course, as your queen, I could order you…"

"Please don't. I would hate to have to disobey. You know I have to do this, Bethan. We can't just sit here merely reacting to everything that fiend decides to throw at us. We *must* take the offensive."

"I know. But why does it have to be you? Why are *you* the one always facing such deadly peril?"

"The prophecy, for one thing, and—"

"And your sense of duty, yes. But I would wish it were otherwise, my love."

"Bethan, I—"

"I don't think there's much point in discussing this any further, do you, Dalveen? Just try not to take any unnecessary risks. For my sake, if nothing else."

"I'll try."

Despite his promise, a shadow hung over the rest of the evening.

* * *

The next day's dawn saw a bustle of activity in and around Torpoint.

One hundred and fifty soldiers had been mustered. They stood by their horses outside the palace's grand entrance. The last of the provisions were being loaded into covered wagons, and secured to the backs of mules.

Leandor always thought of an army preparing to move as a prime example of controlled chaos. This had been no different. But they finally looked ready for departure.

"I still say it's too small a force, lad," Quixwood commented.

"They're the best we have, Golcar, you know that. And there's a lot to be said for a small, well-trained fighting unit going in with determination. Besides, there isn't the time or resources to put together anything bigger. That's your job. Apart from aiding Bethan in running things, I'm relying on you following us with a much larger force within a week."

"Aye, and it will be done. But suppose Avoch-Dar's trying to draw away Delgarvo's defences? His visitations practically inviting you to go to Vaynor could be a trick."

"Perhaps. You'll have to be sure that everything is as secure here as possible before leaving. I know it puts a lot of responsibility on your shoulders, but I'm confident you can do it."

"I'll manage."

"As to it being a trick; our scouts report no movement of troops anywhere in the land. If Avoch-Dar intends a surprise attack, it'll be no surprise by the time it reaches here."

Bethan arrived, attended by several ladies-in-waiting. The crowd parted to allow them through, people bowing on either side.

"I'll make no further attempt to talk you out of this, Dalveen," she told him. "You're too stubborn to take any notice. But I do beg you to take care." She moved forward and embraced him. "Gods speed," she whispered.

"You know in your heart I must do this," he replied softly.

The queen nodded and stepped back.

"Look after her, Golcar," Leandor said after issuing the order for his men to mount.

"You can depend on it. But one last thing. What of Tycho and Shani? Do you want to leave any instructions for them?"

"As we'll be travelling in more or less the same direction, it's possible we'll meet them on the road. Assuming Tycho's found her and they're on their way back. Failing that, tell Tycho that I bid him to stay here and be of service to the Queen. Shani, if she's with him, would also do well to stay until we return."

Leandor mounted his own horse.

He took a last look at Bethan, then signalled his army to move off.

They rode away through streets lined with cheering people.

For more than a day, Drew Hadzor managed to elude the patrols infesting Vaynor. And by his reckoning he should be in sight of Pandemonium at any time.

Now reality was starting to seep in. Having made it this far, he was forced to give serious consideration to what he was actually going to *do*. Because what looked like a good idea in theory was proving somewhat daunting in practice.

The best he could come up with was to scout the area, hoping to find a way of sneaking into the sorcerer's capital. After that, only the gods knew what his next move would be.

Several hours before, rough, scrubby terrain had begun giving way to the edges of desert, and there were no more patches of snow to be seen. Trees, too, were much rarer, having been replaced by jutting outcrops of yellow rock.

He was rounding one of these when he saw the riders. Six men, dressed in black, mounted on black steeds.

Hadzor tried to pull out of sight. But they'd already spotted him. They spurred their horses and galloped his way. He made a run for it.

The monk rode as fast as he dared over that uneven territory. Looking back, they were far enough behind that he dared to hope he would make it.

Then his horse stumbled and fell, throwing him headlong into a patch of gorse. He rolled several times until stopped painfully by a half-buried boulder. The wind was knocked out of him, his head spun.

He was trying to scramble to his feet when the riders arrived. Snaking a hand under his poncho, he pulled out the flail.

They encircled him, grim-faced men with merciless eyes, looking down at him the way hunters regard cornered game. Several dismounted, swords in their hands. He knew resistance was useless and silently cursed himself for getting into such a situation. Still on his knees, he sighed and threw the flail aside.

He was hauled roughly to his feet. Something fell from his clothing. One of the men, presumably their leader, bent and picked it up.

It was the pentagram he had taken after the earlier skirmish. The broken chain still hung from it.

"Our master will want to know how you came by this," the dark rider said. He used the tip of his sword to draw aside Hadzor's open outer garment. And raised an eyebrow at sight of the robes beneath.

"It seems we have some kind of holy man," he announced. "Avoch-Dar will be pleased with such a find."

They mocked Hadzor with disdainful laughter. And dragged the dispirited monk away.

CHAPTER 16

"Are you sure that's all you can remember about Hadzor's theory?" Tycho said.

"Positive," Shani confirmed. "But I don't know if he actually believed it or was just playing with ideas. He seemed serious, though."

In their several days on the road together they had spoken of many things. But the homunculus was particularly intrigued by her account of Drew Hadzor's assertion that the Book of Shadows might somehow be alive.

"It's a fascinating thought," Tycho went on, "although one would need to have a fairly wide definition of the word life."

"You don't think it's such a far-fetched notion, then?"

"Shani, may I remind you that I myself was born of no mortal woman? In fact, I wasn't what you could call *born* at all. I was created from elementary chemicals: an experiment in alchemy to satisfy Avoch-Dar's whim. I have no choice but to believe that life can take many forms."

"I tend to forget that about you. I mean, despite your appearance you seem so…"

"Human? I take that as a compliment. But the fact is I am not. I simply share most of those feelings you humans call emotions. Although whether the sorcerer intended that I should is something I have never been sure about."

"But I'd say emotions are exactly what defines a human. Much more than looks."

"That's an interesting hypothesis, and we could no doubt debate it endlessly. However, my point is that I find it quite conceivable that the book should be a form of life. If a man like Avoch-Dar can create *me*, then think what a so much more advanced race like the demons could achieve."

"Hadzor also thought they might not fully control the tome, remember. Considering how advanced they're supposed to be, is that very likely?"

"Again, I offer myself as an example. I escaped my creator's influence, and he no longer controls me. And when speaking of the demons as being more advanced, I refer to their mastery of magic and other knowledge. I do not believe they are in any way ahead of us morally. Quite the opposite. The myths and legends have always portrayed them as evil entities."

"So the book refused to remain under their influence because they're evil?"

Tycho smiled. "I would not liken the book to myself in that respect, Shani. The demons are wicked; it is logical that their creations should be, too."

"No, it isn't. Avoch-Dar's evil and he created you, but you're not wicked."

"I repeat, he is only a man. He has great magical powers and enormous depravity, but he is still a man for all that. I am convinced that the way I turned out was a mistake. I cannot see the demon race making such an error."

The road swept into a bend, cutting its way through a small wood.

"What of Hadzor's idea that the book's power is neutral, and can be used for good or ill?" Shani said.

"He could be right, but I suspect not. I will stick to my belief that it is malign until there is evidence to the contrary. But we are talking of mysteries that run exceedingly deep. All our speculations may amount to nothing."

"You can say that again." Something ahead caught her attention. "Just a moment, what's happening?"

The sergeant leading their little party had stopped his horse. His hand was raised and he looked back in their direction. Shani and Tycho rode to him.

"What is it?" Tycho asked.

"There, sir." He pointed along the curving trail. A large number of riders were approaching. "Because of the bend in the road, I only just saw them."

"Can you make out who they are?" Shani asked.

"Not at this distance," the sergeant replied. "But at the speed they're travelling, they'll be here in minutes."

"And if we can see them, there's a chance they can see us," Tycho said. "If they're hostile, it could mean trouble. Should we try outrunning them, sergeant?"

"We could only return the way we came, sir, and the road's far too open in that direction. They'd spot us for sure."

"Then all we can do is conceal ourselves in the trees," Shani suggested, "and hope they don't see us."

The pair of troopers at their rear were ordered to hide themselves on one side of the road. Shani, Tycho and the sergeant rode into the undergrowth on the other.

They watched as the riders drew closer. It became obvious a small army was heading their way. Shani fingered her knives, determined to put up some kind of fight should the riders prove hostile.

But when the mounted warriors were near enough for their uniforms to be made out, the sergeant exclaimed, "They're ours!"

And Dalveen's leading them! Shani realized, spurring her horse to the road.

Her companions followed and they galloped to meet the column.

"*Dalveen!*" she yelled.

Leandor looked up. "Shani?" A broad smile spread across his face. He gave the order to halt and reined in his shying horse.

Then she was beside him. "It's so good to see you, Dalveen!"

"And you! It's been too long."

"How do you fare?"

"I'm fine. Bear with me for a moment." He turned to the officer on his other side. "We'll make camp here. Have the men dismount and post lookouts." Returning his attention to her, he said, "We have a lot of catching up to do, Shani."

"You don't know how true that is," she grinned.

Tycho arrived and added his greetings.

"I want to hear all your news," Leandor told them. "And after you've rested and refreshed yourselves, we hold a council of war!"

* * *

The two days Hadzor spent in the dungeons seemed an eternity.

He wasn't even entirely sure it had been two days. Deprived of light, food, water and sound – except sounds he would rather not have heard – it was hard to mark the passage of time.

The monk had reached the point of thinking he was going to be allowed to rot there when guards arrived to drag him out.

They refused to answer any of his questions, indeed to break their silence at all, as he was marched through the palace's gloomy corridors. At length they came to a great hall of black marble. Meagre light from burning brands held back the ocean of darkness.

Hadzor was forced to his knees in front of a man resembling a living corpse, whose very flesh seemed rank with the corruption of evil. A man whose mean features spoke of a wickedness more profound than any the monk had ever seen before.

There was no doubt as to his identity. He could only be the sorcerer.

Avoch-Dar held out a hand that looked like a talon. The medallion Hadzor had taken from the slain rider lay in its palm.

"I'm owed a debt of blood for this," he said.

Hadzor used every grain of will to control his dread.

"You interfered in my plans by siding with Shani Vanya," Avoch-Dar continued, "and I do not take kindly to meddlers."

Hadzor steeled his nerve and replied, "I did only what any man would do when threatened, I fought back."

"And helped take the lives of four of my servants. You frustrated my purpose. Why should I not have you put to death?"

"Because I am in holy orders, perhaps?"

Avoch-Dar mocked him with laughter. "Imbecile! That is all the more reason to take your life. I have a special loathing of your kind. Under my rule, those aligned with the gods will be first for extermination!"

"You will never rule."

"And who's to stop me, monk? You? I think not!"

"It doesn't have to be like this. If you were to fight the evil that's eating at your soul—"

"Oh, please, spare me the sermon!"

"But the power of the book can be used for good! It need not be a force for hatred and destruction!"

"What do you know of the book? By what authority do you pronounce on its nature?"

"I ... I have studied it, read about it. I—"

"You know nothing! Sitting in dusty libraries is one thing, holy man, practical experience is another. As you shall see." He gestured to the guards. "Bring him!"

Avoch-Dar led the way to the centre of the Great Hall. Hadzor was goaded along behind and thrown down before the altar.

He raised his head and looked upon the Book of Shadows.

His fascination outweighed his fear of the sorcerer and he was overawed.

During the years he devoted to the tome he had many times dreamed of one day seeing it. Now the moment had come. And he knew Avoch-Dar was right. No amount of study could prepare him for the sight.

It was plainly of inconceivable antiquity, and the surrounding haze of shimmering blue radiance gave it an eerie aspect. But it wasn't just the book's appearance that was so impressive.

He remembered what Shani had said about her reaction to it. Her description of the way in which she felt it had a kind of intelligence came back to him. And of how disturbing it was to be near the book. For the first time, he truly understood her words.

There was a … presence here. And it wasn't good.

"Now can you possibly doubt its malevolence?" Avoch-Dar asked.

Hadzor could not reply.

"I have made a decision," the wizard announced. "It had been my intention to offer you as a sacrifice. But your connection with Vanya, and through her to Night-shade, makes you more valuable as a hostage."

"I won't co-operate. You may as well kill me and get it over with."

"Co-operate? You have no say in the matter, dolt! Don't delude yourself into thinking I will allow you an easy way out."

"You're the one suffering delusions. Not least your

belief that you can make a pact with the demons with-out paying a terrible price!"

"Ah, so you are an expert on the Sygazon, too." The sorcerer's tone was pure ridicule."

As they spoke, a bulky shape moved towards them through the shadows.

"Whatever they call themselves, they still outrank you by far in evil," Hadzor said, unaware of the approaching figure. "You are dealing with beings that were masters of deception long before humans came into this world."

"Precisely. And for that very reason I could have no better allies. But if you doubt my word, why not put your case to them direct?"

Hadzor was puzzled.

"You have but to look about you," the wizard added, staring beyond the kneeling man.

A chill ran up the monk's spine. Slowly, he turned.

And was faced by the towering obscenity of Lord Berith's frightful body.

He surrendered to terror and screamed.

Night had fallen by the time Leandor's force established camp.

Tents were erected, fires built and sentries posted.

Leandor had his tent put up away from the main encampment, in order not to be disturbed in his deliberations with Shani and Tycho. They settled to eat in front of a fire outside, and to exchange their news, including their thoughts on Drew Hadzor. An hour later they moved on to discussing strategy.

"What exactly *is* your plan once we arrive in Vaynor, Dalveen?" Shani wanted to know.

"As with all campaigns it's best to keep our objectives simple. My aim is to cut off the serpent's head."

"Go directly for Avoch-Dar, you mean?"

"Yes. Either by his capture or his death. I suspect it will take the latter."

"With an army as modest as this? And we'll be fighting on his home ground, remember. Your plan smacks of recklessness."

"A small dedicated group can strike with the precision of a surgeon's knife. Not to mention that the enemy won't expect us to attack this way. I've brought hand-picked men; hardened warriors, all of them. My intention is to adopt guerrilla tactics. I want to avoid a frontal assault at all costs. And Golcar will join us soon with a much larger army."

"Why not wait for him before acting?"

"Because time presses. But have no fear of my taking foolish decisions. If once we get there the odds are too overwhelming, or the defences too strong, we *will* wait for the main army to catch up. See this as an advance force, ready to seize any opportunity presented to us."

"It's a bold scheme," Tycho said, "but does it take into account facing the demons? We have no way of knowing what they might turn on us."

"That's why I'm trying to keep the plan flexible," Leandor replied. Then he smiled and added, "Or to put it another way, making it up as I go along."

"But seriously," Shani interjected, "what happens if we do run into the … Sygazon I think you called them?"

Leandor nodded. "That was the name Melva's shade used. And the honest answer is I don't know. I'd like to avoid contact with them all together, if possible. I'm hoping that once their human ally has been removed, they may withdraw."

"It's a long shot."

"This whole expedition is based on long odds, Shani. That shouldn't stop us trying."

"Agreed. And what of the book? Presumably you intend seizing it, and naturally you'll want to see if it can restore your arm. But what then?"

"We destroy it. Whether it can be made to bring back my arm or not. It's just too dangerous to leave in existence, both in its own right and because it could act as a magnet for the demons again."

"*Can* it be destroyed?"

"Again, I don't know. There are more questions than answers, Shani."

"It's a pity we know nothing more of the weapon

Melva's shade told you about," Tycho remarked. "We could use any help we can get."

"Unfortunately she gave us far too little information to—" He broke off. "Shani, what's wrong?"

She had turned her head away from them and was gazing beyond the fire. There was a curious expression on her face. "Don't know. Can you two hear anything?"

A faint sound was coming from somewhere nearby. It was hard to tell what it might be. Perhaps it was only the rustling of leaves in the evening wind. Perhaps not.

Then an unnatural stillness permeated the air before them.

"I detect a sense of ... *otherness* in the atmosphere," Tycho declared.

Leandor unsheathed his sword as he got up. "It could be another visitation from Avoch-Dar. Keep your wits about you. Tycho, move aside."

Shani drew two knives.

They stood ready.

CHAPTER 17

When a slash of glowing light appeared in the night air just above ground level, Leandor and Tycho guessed what was happening. They relaxed.

"I think this may be friendly," Leandor told Shani.

She was perplexed. "But what…?"

"Watch and see," the homunculus said. "And you may need to shield your eyes at first."

The dazzling line stretched itself like a pair of invisible curtains being drawn apart. Within the widening slit a brilliant golden radiance pulsated; a light too intense for any of them to gaze at directly. They covered their faces with hands and arms.

As it softened, they were able to look again.

A figure stood before them.

Leandor resheathed his sword and stepped forward a pace. "Melva."

"My greetings, Nightshade. And to you, Tycho." The apparition, looking as before like a living person, turned to Shani. "You and I did not meet when I lived. I am pleased to greet you now. And you may put away your knives, my dear."

"Er … yes. Greetings, Melva." It was taking Shani a moment to come to terms with the idea of being spoken to by a dead person, even though Tycho and Dalveen had told her of Melva's earlier visitation. She returned her blades to their scabbards.

Melva favoured them with a sedate smile and explained, "Once the veil of death has been penetrated it makes returning a little easier."

"No need for Karale this time?"

"Her help is no longer necessary. In any event she is engaged with other matters."

Leandor noticed that his soldiers, walking, sitting and sleeping within hailing distance, seemed unaware anything unusual was going on. He assumed Melva's spectre, and the glittering gateway to the Realm of Shades, was visible only to Shani, Tycho and himself.

"Are we doing the right thing in moving against Avoch-Dar?" he asked.

"Evil must be confronted wherever it may be found," Melva replied. "But make no mistake, the way to Vaynor is fraught with danger. Be ever vigilant."

"It might help if I could locate the weapon you spoke of. Can you tell me more?"

"I have learned nothing of its nature. As far as its hiding-place is concerned, you will find it by *not* looking for it. Yet your best chance is to go out of your way."

"I don't understand."

"Moving beyond life has given me insights into many things, but not all. I confess there is much I do not understand myself. What I do know is that although Fate plays a great part in our actions, free will is as important. The gods can aid you by presenting opportunities; your role is in recognizing those chances, grasping them and choosing how to act. It will be so with the weapon."

"You're saying I should keep my eyes open."

"In a way," she smiled. "And to be of flexible mind. It is quite possible you could pass the weapon by without even realizing it. Other gifts from Destiny can likewise be unknowingly missed."

"I will stay alert," he vowed.

"There is a little more to be said of the weapon. It is a heritage of that ancient race I mentioned, which opposes itself to the demons. I told you that the demons' true name is the Sygazon. Now I know this other race to be called the Vitruvius. There is a great mystery surrounding the origin of both races. I cannot define what this puzzle might be, but I believe it is significant. A key, perhaps, to the battle you are engaged in."

"Again you bring me questions, Melva, but few answers."

"At least I bring you the questions! Pursue your destiny and in the fullness of time light may be shed on these riddles. And upon the truth of your own birth, Dalveen."

"Have you discovered something on *that* subject?" he asked eagerly.

"No, not yet. Perhaps never. But lift your head, Nightshade, and be of good spirit. You are doing what you must at last, though the road will be rocky. And be assured that despite encountering problems, Golcar Quixwood makes progress in raising an army. He will follow you shortly."

The oval entrance to the worlds beyond started to pulse once more. Its radiance grew stronger.

"I must leave," the old woman's ghost continued. "Remember this if you forget all else I have said: *beware*. The power of the book is increasing. Make your way to Vaynor with all haste…"

The dazzling gateway embraced her and winked out.

She left her audience dumbfounded.

* * *

Queen Bethan was wrapped in furs to keep out the cold.

She stood with Quixwood on a balcony at Torpoint. Below them, thousands of men and horses filled the main parade ground. Scores of wagons were being loaded.

Quixwood looked exhausted. "Sometimes I think I'm getting too old for this sort of thing," he said.

"Not you," Bethan told him kindly. "You've achieved miracles these past few days. How near are you to departing?"

"Another day or two at least, and that troubles me. It takes us beyond the date I promised Dalveen we'd leave."

"He'll understand. And nobody could have done better in the time available. Don't be like my father, Golcar; not knowing when to ease on your workload and making yourself ill."

"I told Dalveen the same thing, funnily enough. And thank you for your concern, Bethan. But what's important is to be there when he might need us, and an army does not raise itself."

"I'm aware of the problems you've had."

"I should have anticipated them earlier. It's hard enough getting together an army at the best of times, but with our forces depleted from Avoch-Dar's previous invasions, and the shortage of provisions, it's been a nightmare."

"How many men will you be taking?"

"A little over nine thousand. It should be more. A lot more. But we have to leave a sufficiently large enough garrison to defend the city should the need arise."

"Has there been any word from Dalveen?"

"No. But remember he said he'd only send back messengers if there was an emergency. Otherwise he wouldn't want to spare precious men."

"So no messages means he's safe?"

"We assume so."

"Or it could mean—"

"It means he's safe, Bethan, don't fret on that score. Dalveen of all people can look after himself, and he's got the best men we have with him."

"What of Tycho and Shani? Is there news of them?"

"None. But there's a good chance they met Dalveen on the road. His force may be modest, but it would still be hard to miss. I expect they're accompanying him to Vaynor."

"There could be a more sinister reason why we haven't heard. They could all—"

"Stop it. We have no need to believe things aren't going according to plan. It's early days yet. And soon, very soon, I'll be leading out the reinforcements."

"I *hate* this not knowing," Bethan confessed, tears forming in her eyes. "Gods, I'm crying. The Queen can't be seen like this. What will people think of me?" She took a few steps back, away from the faces beneath.

"They will think you human, like themselves, and love you all the more for it."

She pressed herself into his chest and he put his arms around her.

Sobs racked her body.

Leandor, Tycho and Shani talked far into the night, going over everything Melva had said.

As it was obvious none of the troops had witnessed the old woman's visitation, they decided not to mention it to anyone. They had no desire to ignite superstitious fears in the ranks.

The other decision they made was announced at dawn.

When the men were assembled, Leandor mounted his horse to address them.

"As you all know," he said in a loud, clear voice, "our purpose is best served by reaching Vaynor as soon as possible. To achieve this, I have decided to alter the route we'll be travelling. Overland, Vaynor is a week or more away. But we could cut that time in half by making for the sea and coast-hopping to our destination. A small port lies due west of here, and we carry enough gold to acquire the services of a ship."

A murmuring arose, more of approval than protest.

"We leave within the hour," Leandor added. "Make ready. And when we move, proceed with caution. The nearer we get to enemy territory, the more wary we have to be. Dismiss!"

As the crowd dispersed, Leandor slid from his horse and went to Shani and Tycho.

"They took it pretty well, I thought," she said.

"Yes, as soldiers are notorious for disliking changes of plan. But they're well disciplined, as you'd expect from an elite." He turned to the homunculus. "There's something I haven't made clear to you, Tycho."

"Please do, Dalveen."

"I want you to know that you're perfectly at liberty to return to Allderhaven. With an escort, of course. After all, combat isn't first nature with you, my friend, and—"

"Thank you, but no. Apart from the fact that you can't spare the men for an escort, I want to see this through. Unless you're ordering me to return, that is?"

"Absolutely not. I'd very much welcome you staying."

"I may not be a warrior, but I'm sure there are things I can do to help. Indeed, I have one advantage over everybody here. I was brought into being in Vaynor and spent the first part of my life in Pandemonium. It couldn't have changed so much that I won't be able to act as a guide."

"That's settled then," Leandor said, smiling.

"What's the name of this port we're heading for?" Shani asked.

"I'm not too familiar with this part of the realm, but I think it's called Refuge."

"It's likely to be a sheltered bay then. Those little communities can be rather inward looking. Riding in with a hundred and fifty armed men is likely to cause alarm."

"That had occurred to me. I was going to suggest that the troops hold back out of sight while you and I went in to look for a ship."

"Fine by me. Not unlike the first time we met. Remember, Dalveen? In Saltwood, when you were on your way to Zenobia. And so was I, although I didn't know it at the time!"

"After you'd just had that little bit of trouble with the Guild of Thieves."

"Which is one of the reasons those bounty hunters are after us now. You haven't come to regret it, have you? Pitching in on my behalf, I mean."

"Never. I'd do it again tomorrow."

"If I recall correctly," Tycho cut in, "the ship on which you sailed was called *Windrunner*."

"That's right," confirmed Leandor. "An attractive vessel she was, too. Good looking. Sleek."

"And she went down with all hands," Tycho said.

"*Thanks* for the reminder," Shani hissed, glaring at him.

"I was merely reminiscing too."

"Sometimes, Tycho, you have all the sensitivity of a mountain bear with a thorn in its paw. I don't know why you don't join the diplomatic service! And what are *you* grinning at, Dalveen?"

She snatched up her saddle and made for the horses.

"Oh, come on, you two," she called over her shoulder, "let's get moving!"

CHAPTER 18

They rode steadily for half the day. Their trail ran beside an icy stream, sloping downward at a gentle gradient through hilly terrain with a generous scattering of trees. No snow had fallen that morning, but the sun was too weak to melt the existing white patches.

At around midday they came to a small valley, framed by steep hills. Leandor called a halt to get his bearings and took out a folded map.

"How far now?" Shani wanted to know.

"Once we get through there," he replied, nodding at the valley's mouth, "we should be well on our way to the ocean."

"Let's go then."

"Just a minute." He studied the map. "According to this, the area we'll be entering is part marshland. I don't want us getting bogged down in it, especially the wagons. So I'll send out some scouts to check the ground."

Four men were ordered to ride a short distance ahead. The rest of the force followed at a trot.

Tycho was riding at Leandor's side. After a while he said, "That's curious."

"What is?"

"The birds. They've been singing all morning, but for the last ten minutes or so it's gone absolutely quiet. Hadn't you noticed?"

"No, I— *Gods!*" He turned in his saddle and barked at the officer behind him. "Stop the column and take up defensive positions! And get those scouts back!"

The man was mystified. "But, sir—"

"Do it *now!*"

An order went rapidly down the line. Two troopers galloped off to warn the advance party. Swords were drawn, shields raised. The supply wagons formed a circle and the pack mules led into it. Everyone scanned the surrounding countryside.

There was total silence, except for the sound of the hooves of the horses ridden by the men going for the scouts.

"Where are the enemy?" Tycho wondered.

"*There!*" Shani exclaimed, pointing to the top of

the hill on the valley's right.

"*And there!*" the officer shouted. He pointed to the opposite ridge.

Black uniformed riders on black steeds were pouring over the crests of the hills and down into the valley.

"Thanks to you, Tycho, we just avoided riding into a trap," Shani said.

"Don't expect them to give up," Leandor told her. "There's still going to be a fight!"

The scouts were already heading back at speed, and the two men sent after them were also retreating. Scores of dark riders thundered in hot pursuit.

Shouts of encouragement rose from the Delgarvian army.

As the six troopers raced for their lives, more enemy cavalry appeared from the treeline on either side of the valley.

"There's at least as many of them as there are of us," Shani reckoned. "What do we do, Dalveen? Charge them?"

"No. Let them tire *their* horses."

A cheer went up around them. The six troopers were home safe, their pursuers having slowed to a canter. Leandor knew they were only waiting for the rest of their force to catch up. Then there would be a full-scale attack.

"Tycho, I want you out of here," he ordered. "Take yourself over to the circle of wagons."

"Yes, Dalveen. Good luck, you two!" The homunculus spurred his horse and galloped away.

Leandor drew his blade. "If I were you, Shani, I'd use a sword and keep your knives in reserve. You'll find it serves better in a mounted battle."

She reached for the scabbard attached to her saddle and pulled out a sabre.

"Happy with that?" he asked.

The blade swished cleanly as she cut a practice swipe. "It's sharp. I'm happy."

"Here they come!" the officer shouted.

The black riders advanced. They were working up to a charge.

Leandor raised himself in his saddle. *"Spread out, men!"* he yelled. *"And stand your ground!"*

"Any last minute advice?" Shani said.

"Kill as many as you can."

"I'll try to remember that," she replied dryly.

The first line of charging riders was now no further than a spear throw away. Some of them bellowed war cries. Leandor's troops put out an answering chorus.

In seconds, the enemy were near enough to make out individual faces, twisted with blood-lust.

Then they met the Delgarvian ranks and all hell broke loose.

A great roar went up from warriors on both sides. The air filled with the sounds of shouts, clashing steel, screaming men and horses.

Leandor's first opponent managed a single stroke before taking a lethal blow to his chest. The second was knocked from his saddle by the impact of a shoulder wound. The third went down with a ribbon of scarlet across his throat.

Ducking a sword swing, Shani sliced into an attacker's leg. He yelled, pulling away into the throng, and was immediately replaced by another raider. They crossed blades twice. Her third swipe raked the side of his face. He fell shrieking into the confusion of milling hooves. The next man came near to taking her head. She plunged the sabre into his belly.

All around, bodies of friend and foe littered the churned, slushy earth.

The officer nearest Leandor slumped forward, stabbed in the back. Leandor's sword swiftly repaid his killer.

More dark riders swept into the Delgarvian lines.

Taken unawares, Shani barely avoided a blade aimed at her neck. She beat off her assailant and felled him. But the next struck her sabre hard enough to part her from it. The weapon spiralled away and was lost.

A pair of raiders boxed in Leandor, one on each side. He lashed out at the man on his left, dumping him from his horse. Then he cut to the right, but his blow was wide. They fenced hard and it took Leandor four passes to get through the man's defences. He pierced his heart.

Leandor caught a glimpse of Shani. She was struggling to control her rearing horse, and he saw she no longer had her sword. Then he was sucked back into the furious tumult.

Shani couldn't calm the steed. Bucking wildly, it threw her and bolted. Softened mud cushioned the fall, and she was fortunate there were no other horses nearby to trample her. As she climbed to her feet and looked around for a riderless mount, her luck soured further.

Assuming she was easy pickings, a black clad horseman raced toward her.

But she had her knives. Quickly snatching one, she launched it with all her strength. The blade struck the charging man squarely and he toppled from sight. His horse wheeled and made for the open plain.

She had to expend another knife on a second rider who tried the same thing. At this rate she was going to run out of blades before she ran out of targets. She needed a horse and a sword. Fast.

A steed galloped past with a corpse draped over it. She leapt to grab the flapping reins but couldn't quite reach. The spooked animal disappeared into the scrum, leaving her cursing.

Leandor was too preoccupied to notice Shani's plight. He'd spent precious minutes fending off a man armed with an axe and shield. A dogged opponent, the man attacked without let and rarely dropped his defences.

His fatal mistake came when drawing back the axe too far. Leandor instantly sent his sword into the raider's exposed armpit, then finished him with a backhand swipe to the chest.

Shani was at the point of considering a dash for the wagons when an enemy's horse brushed against her side. The rider was busy exchanging blows with a trooper. She took hold of his leg and pulled, tugging with all her weight. The shocked man directed a swipe at her head, lost balance and plunged to the ground.

Winded, he put up no resistance as she wrenched the sword from his hand. Determined not to lose the chance of gaining his horse, she jumped over him and snatched a stirrup. That stilled the beast long enough for her to get a hold on its reins and speedily mount.

Vicious hand-to-hand combat still boiled all around, and the air was rent with blood-curdling screams, but it seemed to her that the fighting was dying down. The impression was confirmed when she saw several score of the enemy riding away from the battle.

She sought out Leandor. He was nearby, duelling with a pair of riders, one brandishing a two-handed sword. Shani urged her steed that way.

Arriving at a gallop, she took one of the men by surprise and dislodged him with a single, arcing slice. His companion, with the two-hander, was distracted for a split second. Enough for Leandor to drive his blade between the man's ribs and be rid of him.

Dalveen saluted her with his sword. "Thanks, Shani!"

"My pleasure. You think we've got the better of them?"

"Yes, they're routed. Look."

The enemy raiders were in full retreat, most making for the valley and adjacent trees.

"But let's make sure and see them off," he added, raising his sword above his head. "*To me, Delgarvians!*" he yelled. "*To me!*"

His soldiers heeded the call and disengaged from the few fights still going on. They rode to him from all directions.

Then he was leading them in a charge, Shani at his side, pounding across the countryside in pursuit of the fleeing riders. When they reached the entrance to the valley, and only a few stragglers were still in sight, he called a halt.

Having satisfied themselves that the danger was over, and the trees hid no reserves, they headed back to the scene of battle.

Tycho was put in charge of damage assessment.

Others groups were assigned to tend the wounded, gather weapons and round up horses.

Several hours later, the homunculus reported to Leandor.

"Almost a third of our number are dead. Add to that the wounded and we'll be left with less than a hundred men. Ninety-one, to be precise."

"*That* high a toll?" Leandor said. "It's a heavy blow, Tycho."

"We gave a good account of ourselves," Shani remarked. She was cleaning her retrieved knives and returning them to their scabbards. "I'd say we killed twice as many of them."

"Our troopers did well," Leandor agreed. "But we've been deprived of a lot of fine men today and can ill afford the loss."

Tycho seated himself on an up-ended barrel. "The question is, do we have a large enough force to carry on? Numbers were tight to start with; things are going to be that much harder now."

"I'm determined to keep going," Leandor resolved. "If we turn back, we lose the time advantage of striking now. Perhaps more important is what it would do to morale. We'd run the risk of defeatism spreading throughout Delgarvo."

"Unfortunately, we have also discarded the option of waiting for Golcar's reinforcements until we reach Vaynor," Tycho reminded them. "He does not know we have taken a different route."

"You're right. But I'm not wasting the lives of more good soldiers by ordering them to carry messages through terrain swarming with Avoch-Dar's riders. So for the time being we're on our own."

"I suppose there is no doubt who these riders were acting for?" Tycho asked, indicating the battleground with a fuzzy hand.

Shani dug something out of her pocket. "If there were, I think this decides the issue." She held out a black pentagram medallion. "All the enemy dead have them."

"Identical to the ones my bodyguards were found to be wearing," Leandor said.

"And the men Hadzor and I encountered."

"Well, despite our modest numbers, it seems we should take heart," Tycho declared.

Shani was puzzled. "Why?"

"Because Avoch-Dar is obviously so worried about us that he'll go to any lengths to bring about our deaths."

"Excuse me if I don't feel flattered," she told him wryly.

CHAPTER 19

Hadzor was made to witness the ambush.

He feared the Delgarvians would be wiped out. Avoch-Dar's boasting had certainly lead him to believe that was going to happen. But the monk had watched with increasing elation as the sorcerer's black-garbed followers were beaten and repelled.

Now the viewing pool showed their bodies strewn about the battlefield.

The Sygazon's representative, Berith, was present. Hadzor still hadn't come to terms with the demon lord's hideous appearance. Nor did the all-pervasive air of evil the creature projected seem any less disturbing. And it was impossible to read its moods.

So Hadzor wasn't surprised that what passed for Berith's face gave no hint of a reaction to the defeat.

On the other hand there was nothing unreadable about Avoch-Dar's response.

The wizard was beside himself with fury. He raged, cursed and shrieked dire threats, swearing to consign Nightshade's soul to the infernal realms.

When he began to calm down, the demon finally addressed the sorcerer. "You have failed again," it wheezed unpleasantly. "The Sygazon expect better of their ... allies. You have thrown away the lives of your men. It would have been preferable to feed their souls to the book."

Berith's remark hinted at the terrible fate humans faced if the Sygazon succeeded in taking back the world.

"Nightshade and his little army will be destroyed long before they reach Vaynor," the sorcerer promised. "As to feeding the book, there is no danger of the supply of life essences running short. Allow me to demonstrate."

Berith snorted in what Hadzor took to be a sign of agreement.

The wizard nodded to a guard and the man hurried from the hall. Seconds later he returned, leading a bound prisoner. White with terror, she was prostrated before the altar. The blue radiance flowing around the Book of Shadows started to throb.

Unable to stay silent, Hadzor spoke up. "You cannot do this, Avoch-Dar!" he protested. The guards at his back painfully tightened their hold.

"Silence!" the wizard snapped. "I can still change my mind about you!"

"Take my life in her stead, if you must. But in the name of the gods, show mercy!"

"How very noble of you," Avoch-Dar replied scornfully. "Now hold your tongue or prepare to lose it!"

The monk looked on helplessly as tendrils of energy snaked from the book.

And wished that he could block out the sacrifice's dreadful screams.

The Delgarvians took the rest of the day burying their dead and preparing to set off again. Leandor considered spending the night at the battle site and starting afresh next morning, but decided to lose no more precious time.

It was early evening when they resumed their journey. A handful of the brighter stars were already visible in the winter sky, along with the outline of a crescent moon. To give warning of any further attacks, extra lookouts were positioned ahead, to the rear and on both flanks of the column.

They travelled uneventfully, and several hours later found themselves on the top of a hill overlooking Refuge's twinkling lights. Beyond the small port town the great dark mass of the ocean stretched to an invisible horizon. The sound of crashing waves could be heard.

Leandor's new second-in-command, an older sergeant hardened by a lifetime's campaigning, suggested they make camp in a nearby wood.

"Sounds a good idea," Leandor agreed. "But maintain silence and light no fires. I don't want us attracting attention. Post sentries and tell them to stay out of sight."

"What is your plan, Dalveen?" Tycho asked.

"There's no point wasting time. Shani and I are going down there now. We'll take some bags of gold coin and hope there's a ship to be purchased."

"Will you be wanting an escort, sir?" the sergeant said.

"No. A group of strangers could arouse suspicions." He looked to Tycho. "And that's the reason I want you to stay here too, old friend."

"I understand. My appearance would certainly arouse suspicions, and perhaps hostility."

"Are we hiring a crew as well?" Shani wanted to know.

"Only if we have to settle for a vessel that needs expert handling. Otherwise I'd prefer not to involve outsiders. We have one or two men here with seafaring experience. And we'll be staying in sight of the coast the whole way; it's not as though we'll be heading out to sea."

"That's a risk, but I expect we'll manage. But what do we do if there are no ships to be had?"

"Then we'll have to consider taking one. Our mission's too important to abandon at this stage. Are you ready?"

Shani nodded.

"One question, sir," the sergeant said. "What happens if you run into trouble down there?"

"If we're not back in, say, four hours, you have my permission to send in a rescue party. In the event of our deaths, Tycho here assumes command. He'll make overall decisions. You, sergeant, will be in charge of military strategy. Whether you decide to go on or return to Allderhaven is down to you, Tycho."

"It is a great responsibility, Dalveen."

"I know you'll do the right thing. But don't worry about us. I think we can look after ourselves."

For a small port, Refuge turned out to be surprisingly busy.

As Leandor and Shani rode in, they found the narrow streets filled with people. Loaded wagons, and strings of mules carrying goods, added to the congestion. Every tavern seemed full to bursting.

"More than one ship must have berthed here recently," Leandor reckoned.

"Then we're in luck," Shani said. "It increases our chances of finding one that's available. And we should be less conspicuous in this crowd."

"Like Tycho, it takes more than a crowd to make *me* inconspicuous."

"That cloak serves well enough in concealing your empty sleeve. Come on, let's get down to the harbour."

If it had not been for the number of people thronging the streets, Leandor and Shani might have noticed the pair of riders following them at a distance. But the man and woman would probably have been hard to spot even if the town was deserted. They were experts in the art of tracking, professional stalkers of human prey.

Both were dressed plainly in order not to draw attention to themselves. The various weapons each carried were discreetly concealed. Even the horses they rode displayed no finery in tackle or grooming.

The woman's long red tresses had been pleated into a single strand and tucked into the neck of her buttoned jerkin. She wore a simple, wide-brimmed felt hat, the better to hide her striking features.

The man favoured an unadorned headband to hold his lengthy black hair in place. He was clean shaven, though a beard would have helped disguise one feature marring a face that could otherwise be called handsome. An old scar, deep and unsightly, ran from just below his left eye, down through the corner of his mouth and to the tip of his chin.

"What do you think they're up to?" the woman wondered.

"I've no idea."

"I say that if they lead us anywhere with less of a mob about we seize the opportunity to strike."

"Patience, Jocasta. Leandor in particular is not to be underestimated. We must choose the time and place with great care. It seems Hobbe acted on impulse, and look what happened to him."

"He was a dolt."

"It's fortunate for us he was. One less rival to contend with and only ourselves to share the bounty."

"I'd have thought you would have done this job for the sheer pleasure of it, never mind the reward."

"Oh, certainly. But a fat purse at the end of our task will make victory all the sweeter."

"Just don't keep me waiting too long. My way is to act when the chance arises. I'm not used to working with anyone else and having to consult on every move."

"This is the first time I've ever taken a partner myself, you know that. But then Nightshade is a special case. And Vanya is no ordinary opponent either, as I believe you discovered."

"She's … pretty good," the woman grudgingly admitted.

The man smiled. "Nowhere near as skilful as you, of course." His tone was slightly mocking. Her eyes flared darkly, but before she could voice her offence he added, "All I ask is that Leandor be left to me. He's *mine*, understand?"

"Whatever you say. I'm more concerned to settle a score with her."

"Good. Let's keep it that way."

He ran his fingers down the scar and stared intently at Leandor's back.

Once they arrived at the quay, Dalveen and Shani began making enquiries about ships for sale. The first one they were directed to turned out to be a large fishing boat, totally unsuitable for carrying nearly a hundred men, horses and provisions.

Then someone suggested they speak to an old man who had a three-mast merchant clipper moored at the other end of the quay. It was called *Ocean Ranger*.

They found him sitting on a hawser smoking a briar pipe. He was ancient and weather-beaten, with white whiskers and a bald dome. Explaining that he was only selling the ship because he was retiring, he invited them to step aboard.

The vessel looked even older than its master, but as far as Shani and Leandor could see, it was basically sound. Not wanting to let on that they knew next to nothing about ships, lest the price be based on their ignorance, they refrained from asking too many questions. They spent most of the inspection listening to the owner's sales pitch. Then they followed him around the deck, occasionally stopping to rap their knuckles against a piece of woodwork in what they hoped was a knowing kind of way.

Shani had the presence of mind to ask if they could see below decks. The old man showed them how to get there and left them to it.

"What are we supposed to be doing down here?" Leandor whispered.

"*I* don't know," she hissed back. "Looking to see if there are any holes or anything, I suppose."

"If there were, presumably the thing would have sunk by now."

"Oh, you know what I mean! Truth is, I haven't a clue what we're supposed to be looking for, and neither have you. You said some of the troopers had seafaring experience. We should have brought one of them with us."

"Maybe. But I wanted to keep this little excursion simple, remember? Anyway, it's just a matter of common sense. All we need is a ship that will serve for one short voyage in which the shore is never going to be out of sight. It needs to be big enough to carry our men, the horses and some supplies."

"What about the wagons?"

"They'll have to be left behind. Along with the spare horses and mules. We're travelling light from now on."

"In that case this should be fine for us." She slapped her hand against the hull. It came away covered in green slime. "I think."

They went back up and started haggling over money. An hour later they agreed a price that was higher than Leandor was entirely happy with, but much lower than the outrageous figure the old sea dog had originally demanded. The arrangement was half in gold now, the balance when they returned to collect.

"When will that be?" the seller asked.

"In two or three hours," Leandor replied.

"You want it that quickly?"

"We need to set sail with the morning tide. Is that a problem?"

"No. It just seems a bit of a hurry, that's all. What about your crew? Do you need to do any hiring?"

"We have our own crew. They'll be with us when we come back."

"Where are you bound?"

"Just a little way along the coast for a trading trip."

"You're merchants?"

"Er, yes."

He didn't look very convinced. "You're not familiar with the waters in these parts, are you?"

"Not really," Leandor admitted.

"Well, if you take my advice you'll stay as close to the shoreline as you can. Whatever you do, don't go near Nordelph. There's trouble on the island and you're best keeping well from it."

"Nordelph's just a name to me," Shani confessed. "What's the story?"

"It's a self-proclaimed island state," Leandor explained, "though there's always been a dispute about whether it falls under Delgarvo law or not. It's been ruled by a series of despots for decades."

"Aye," the old man interjected, "and now it's got a new one. Keez Mylius, he calls himself, and he's been running the place for about a year. He's the worst they've ever had. Rules with an iron hand, he does. Things have got so bad there's a rebel force trying to overthrow him. Wouldn't be surprised if there was civil war over there before too long."

"We'll be sure to avoid it," Shani told him. "Thanks for the tip."

He saw them down the gangplank and on to their horses. They rode off.

The old man went and sat on his hawser again. Smiling, he started to refill his pipe.

A man and woman walked over to him. They engaged him in conversation. The woman pointed in the direction Leandor and Shani had gone. Her companion dropped some coins into the old man's palm.

It was proving a profitable day for *Ocean Ranger*'s ex-master. Now *these* people were paying him to answer questions about *those* people. At this rate he'd have a tidy nest egg to take into retirement with him.

CHAPTER 20

Leandor returned to Refuge just after midnight. He brought a skeleton crew of ten men with him, dressed in civilian clothes. Shani stayed with the main force, who would use the cover of darkness to make their way along the coast to an agreed pick-up point.

The old sea captain was paid the remainder of his gold. He left without mentioning the pair of visitors who had come to him earlier.

There was little rest for Leandor and his men that night. Their time was spent getting *Ocean Ranger* ready for departure at dawn. They checked the rigging and sails, carefully inspected the hull for leaks and took on an ample supply of fresh water. It was the small hours before they were satisfied the ship was seaworthy.

They caught the morning tide, managing to navigate around the other berthed ships without too much difficulty. Soon the port was behind them and they unfurled all sails for the first stage of their journey.

Not much more than an hour later they arrived at the quiet cove where their companions were waiting, dropping anchor as near the shore as they dared. Troopers appeared from hiding, poured down the sandy beach and began wading out to the ship. They led horses and carried boxes of provisions.

Another hour saw everyone aboard and the supplies secured below decks. Priority had been given to food, weapons and basic medical needs. The wagons and remaining provisions were left in a nearby wood. All they could do with the surplus horses and unwanted mules was release them into the wild.

At mid-morning they set off on their coastal voyage. Leandor reckoned they should reach their destination within the day.

Once they were under way there was little to do other than trying to catch up on sleep. Sitting on the deck, Leandor, Shani and Tycho took the opportunity to go over some recent events they hadn't had a chance to discuss.

Shani was especially interested in what Melva's ghost had said about there being another ancient race. "What did she call them? The Vitruvius?"

"I think so," Leandor said flatly.

"You don't seem too excited about it, Dalveen. Surely the existence of another race as strong as the Sygazon, and opposed to them, has got to be good news?"

"Perhaps. But I don't see that we can jump to conclusions based on such scant information. I mean, where are they? *What* are they? For all we know they could have died out aeons ago."

"That wasn't the impression I got from the way Melva referred to them. She seemed to think this Vitruvius could have a part to play in coming events."

"They may be opposed to the Sygazon, but that doesn't necessarily mean they're any less evil."

"'My enemy's enemy is my friend'," Shani quoted, "and we can use all the help going."

"What Melva told us is far too vague. I prefer something solid to work on, like the location of that weapon she mentioned. And to be frank, the thought that I might get involved with unleashing another powerful inhuman race on the world isn't a prospect I relish. It's bad enough knowing it's my fault the demons returned."

"It is not rational to blame yourself for that, Dalveen," Tycho chipped in.

"On the contrary, it's hard to see it any other way. If I hadn't found the book, and if I hadn't let it fall into Avoch-Dar's hands—"

"If, if, if," Shani interrupted. "For a start, you're ignoring the prophecy, which at least implied that you were born to search for the book."

"I'd say the prophecy only promised me a *chance* to find the book; and it carried no guarantees about what would happen afterwards. You're not taking into account the element of free will Melva spoke of. It was the decisions I made, based on my free will, that got us into this whole mess."

"Maybe, maybe not. We're all agreed that the book represents a mystery far deeper than any of us yet understands. I keep thinking of what Drew Hadzor said. He was foolhardy, and he was certainly obsessed, but he'd obviously given a lot of thought to the subject. There might just be something in his theory that the book's powers are neither inherently good *or* evil."

"I think his ideas are muddle-headed. But perhaps I should have found the time to speak with him."

"It could be his ideas aren't so stupid. If you'd managed to retain the book, you would have tried using it for good, wouldn't you? Had it restored your arm that would have been a positive thing, surely? Hadzor thought it possible that the nature of the person controlling the book determined whether it was a good or bad force. What's so far-fetched about that?"

"But the book *didn't* restore my arm, and it achieved precious little in the way of good while it was in our possession."

"It healed the wound Kreid gave you," she reminded him, "and it got us back to Delgarvo. And it could be it didn't restore your arm simply because we didn't know how to use it properly."

Leandor sighed. "As you said, Shani, it's all a mystery. For the time being I'm putting faith in my sword and the fighters with us. I'm not thinking beyond dealing with the sorcerer and destroying the damn book."

"What is that?" Tycho said, changing the topic.

They looked beyond the rail and out to sea. A long black strip of land could be seen sitting on the horizon.

"Must be Nordelph," Leandor replied. "The island we were warned to avoid."

"You said it's been ruled by dictators for years," Shani remarked. "Why didn't King Eldrick do anything about it?"

"He always meant to. But there were those doubts about whether it fell under Delgarvo's jurisdiction, and sending an expeditionary force could have been too costly in lives. Plus, its rulers were never openly hostile to us."

"If the man who sold us this ship was telling the

truth, the new ruler over there... What was his name?"

"Keez Mylius."

"This Mylius sounds a dreadful tyrant. I'm surprised you're content to let him get away with it, Dalveen."

"I'm not. It's something I intend rectifying, like Bearsden, once our present business is over. Assuming we return alive, of course."

"I'm glad to hear it."

"But put Nordelph from your mind," he told her. "It doesn't concern us for the moment, fortunately, and we'll be staying well away."

Avoch-Dar took an unholy pleasure in taunting Hadzor. If he wasn't insulting or threatening the monk, he was making him watch unpleasant scenes, as now.

Hadzor was lashed to one of the marble columns in Pandemonium's Great Hall. It was a column nearest to the viewing pool, and he could clearly see its bubbling surface.

The sorcerer and Berith were gazing into the churning green liquid, too. And Avoch-Dar was conjuring a spell.

An image came into focus. It was of a ship at sea, its triple-masted sails swelling with wind. Another pass of the wizard's talon-like hands wiped the picture away and replaced it with something else.

Leandor, Shani Vanya and the homunculus, Tycho,

sitting together on the ship's deck. In the background, Delgarvian troopers were crewing the vessel.

"The nearer he gets," Berith hissed, "the more certain it is our power will affect him."

"Mark this well, holy man," the wizard sneered. "You are about to see the great Nightshade come to grief!"

"Go on," Berith urged. "With your skills and the additional powers we have bestowed upon you, the conjuration should prove simple."

Avoch-Dar made a series of complicated gestures.

The image in the pool faded again, then returned to the original perspective. It showed the ship from a distance. The sails appeared a little fuller, and the hull was rocking a fraction more than it had previously.

In the foreground the waves seemed to be growing choppier.

On *Ocean Ranger*'s deck, Leandor and the others were interrupted by a shout from the crow's nest.

The lookout was pointing, not seaward, but inland.

Far above the hilly coast a mass of angry black clouds was forming. Searing streaks of lightning illuminated their interiors. A stiff wind was already beginning to reach the ship.

Shani stared at the ominous gathering of clouds in puzzlement. "Where did *that* come from?"

"Apparently some of these freak storms can blow up without warning," Leandor said.

"Yes, but over the sea, surely, not the land?"

"I'm not an expert on the weather, Shani. I'm only concerned with whether it will affect us."

"I think you can assume it will," Tycho commented. "It definitely seems to be coming our way."

Leandor felt a smattering of salt spray against his face. "You're right," he agreed. "*Sergeant!*"

His second-in-command arrived smartly and snapped a brisk, "Sir?"

"It looks like we're in for some rough conditions. Trim those sails. Have any loose cargo tied down and make sure the horses are secured. All men with no business on deck should get themselves below. And I want that lookout down from the crow's nest."

"*Yes, sir!*" The sergeant hurried off to relay his orders.

"I'm going up to the bridge," Leandor announced.

Shani and Tycho followed him. The wind was building. Already the vessel was beginning to roll.

The trooper with the most seafaring experience had been assigned the wheel. Leandor strode over to consult him.

"Ever seen anything like this before?"

"No, sir. Not coming from inland, anyway. That's more the kind of storm you'd expect to see blowing up well out to sea."

"Do we drop anchor or what?" Shani asked.

"That's not a good idea this close to shore," the man replied. "The winds coming at us are likely to be made stronger as they funnel over those cliffs yonder. If we were anchored the force could tear us apart."

"So we try to ride it out?" Leandor said.

"Yes, sir. But I could do with some help controlling the wheel if things get really bad."

"I'll be staying with you."

"And us," Shani insisted, speaking for herself and the homunculus.

Leandor had better things to do than argue. "All right. But if you're staying, it'd be a good idea to tie yourself to something."

Waves started to break over the deck below, soaking the men struggling to lower the sails.

Rope was produced and they lashed the helmsman to the wheel. Leandor took up position next to him. He ran a loop around his waist and knotted it through the hand grip on top of the rail. Further back, Shani and Tycho did the same thing.

Without warning an enormous wave struck *Ocean Ranger*'s port side. The ship rocked violently. Torrents of rain plunged down from the black clouds, now almost directly overhead. Lightning flashed and thunder boomed.

Another wave hit, even bigger, and through the deluge they saw several men washed across the deck below. At least two disappeared over the side.

"I'm having trouble holding her!" the helmsman yelled.

Leandor added the weight of his arm to the wheel, the muscles standing out on his shoulder and back.

A further, larger wave came in, clearing the deck of the remaining men and cargo.

The ship was being forced out to sea, and nothing they could do would stop it.

All around it was black as night. Mountainous waves pummelled them ceaselessly. They held on for dear life, totally helpless in the face of the savage tempest.

CHAPTER 21

It was hard to tell how much time passed before the storm spent itself. But slowly the wind died down, the waves lessened and quiet returned.

Ocean Ranger was completely becalmed, and far out at sea. The mainland couldn't be seen. Nordelph was still visible, and somewhat closer, but still a long way off.

The sergeant reported to Leandor. "Seven men lost, sir, and a handful injured, mostly not too serious, fortunately. Quite a bit of the deck cargo went and the forward mast was badly damaged. Several of the sails are ripped and the rigging's in a mess, although that can be fixed. I suppose it could have been a lot worse, sir."

"I suppose it could, sergeant. Thank you."

The man went about his business. Shani came over.

"We've checked below," she said, "and at least we're not shipping any water. Though I think that's more down to luck than anything else."

"It was only pure luck we weren't sent to the bottom," Leandor added.

"I'll be damned if that storm was natural, Dalveen. I've spoken to a couple of the men who had time at sea and they agree with me. Apart from anything else it came on far too fast."

"It had to be a gift from our friend the sorcerer, didn't it? And the ironic thing is that now we're helpless for *want* of some wind."

"Won't we eventually drift back to shore, anyway?" asked Shani.

"Not this far out. As a matter of fact the currents are gradually taking us further away from land."

"Well, there's not much we can do about it except hope for the best and wait."

For two and a half hours they did just that. And it wasn't the arrival of wind that had the lookout calling down to them.

They scanned the seaward horizon.

"There!" Leandor said, pointing to a distant speck. "A sail."

The white square grew larger in a matter of

minutes. Soon it was possible to see something of the vessel itself.

"How come they're travelling at such a speed when we can't move at all?"

"Because they're not relying on wind power. See?" He pointed. "Along both sides of its hull."

Shani squinted at the approaching ship. "Oars?"

"Yes. And there are three classes of craft that operate with oarsmen: warships, prison ships and pirate ships."

"Care to have a guess at which it might be?"

"In theory, it could be any one of them. But if it's a warship I can't imagine whose, in these waters. Same thing applies to a floating prison. I'm pretty sure there aren't supposed to be any around here."

"Leaving pirates?"

"It's a distinct possibility. We're not too far from the Amrac Islands, and that's a free port for buccaneers and bootleggers."

"The Amracs are much further south, surely?"

"We're drifting south, as a matter of fact. And pirate ships range far and wide in this part of the world."

"Ships with oarsmen only fall into these three categories?"

"Oh, yes. For a very simple reason. No one would willingly choose to make up a crew of rowers on an ocean-going vessel. It's backbreaking, and often fatal. So oarsmen are always enforced labour."

"Slaves, you mean."

He nodded. "Prisoners of war, convicts and pirate captives."

"*Great*. This is just what we need, Dalveen."

"We'll have to assume they're hostile and be prepared. Unfortunately, we don't have the option of trying to outrun them."

"And at the rate they're moving they'll be here in no time."

Leandor ordered everyone on deck and explained the situation. Extra weapons were issued. Troopers took up positions along the length of the ship.

In thirty minutes, the oared galleon was near enough that they could make out its figurehead: a red dragon with gold-tipped talons and a curling green tail.

The ship bore no name and was half again as big as the *Ocean Ranger*. Its decks and rigging were crowded with men, easily a hundred or more, with many pressing against the rails. They bristled with cutlasses.

"They're flying no flag that I can see," the sergeant observed.

No sooner had he said it than a standard was run up the mast. When it reached the top there was just enough of a breeze to let it open out. It was black, with white markings. The markings formed an image universally recognized, and that left no doubt who these seamen were.

The profile of a wolf, its mouth open and fangs exposed.

"That settles it," Shani said. "The pirate ensign!"

The raiding ship was pulling about, so that in a few seconds its starboard side would be parallel with theirs.

Leandor stepped on to a barrel and raised his sword above his head. *"Delgarvians!"* he yelled. *"Prepare to repel boarders!"*

Standing in the open air on top of one of the palace's towers, Bethan and Quixwood looked down at the assembled army.

"All is ready?" she said.

"Yes, finally. We leave within the hour."

"I shall miss you, Golcar. Your advice and support have sustained me."

"We'll be back before you know it. And you have plenty of good counsellors here to aid you in the meantime."

"None as trustworthy or as wise as you."

"Thank you, Bethan. Now I really must be—"

"Hold for one second, Golcar Quixwood."

The unexpected interruption surprised them. They spun around. Quixwood's hand went to his sword.

"Karale!" Bethan exclaimed.

Melva's granddaughter smiled. "I'm sorry if I startled you, Your Majesty."

Quixwood was baffled. "How did you get up here? It shouldn't have been possible to pass the number of guards we have posted."

"Anything is possible if needs must," she replied mysteriously. "But I will not waste time trying to explain. The reason for my coming is more important."

"You have news of Dalveen?" Bethan asked anxiously.

"He is alive, as are Shani and Tycho. Some of their company have not been so fortunate."

"There's been trouble? What happened?" Quixwood demanded.

"I am not my grandmother; I have merely a fraction of her farsight. For me, events at a distance come only as vague, general impressions. So I cannot be specific about the perils they face."

"Can't Melva herself come to us and tell more?" Bethan suggested.

"Not now. She is watching over Nightshade and his comrades as best she can, and that is as much as she can do from the Realm of Shades."

"What *can* you tell us?" Quixwood said.

"Two things. The first may not seem necessary, but hear me anyway. Move with as much speed as you can muster, Golcar, and do not be tempted to linger anywhere along the way. Expect opposition before you reach Vaynor. Avoch-Dar's forces range further afield than you suspect. And once you reach your destination do not expect Nightshade to be there to meet you."

"*My gods,*" Bethan whispered. "You mean—"

"I do not wish to imply that death will prevent him being there. Although I must be honest and say that it could. Be brave, my Queen. I repeat, he lives now. And he is a favourite of the gods. I tell you this only so that Golcar can be prepared to act on his own initiative, if need be."

"I don't like the sound of it, girl," Quixwood told her, "but I appreciate the warning. What was the other thing you had to tell us?"

"In a way it is even more vital. Avoch-Dar grows stronger through his alliance with the Sygazon and the unfolding of the book's secrets. They are about to take more of a hand in determining events. Beware deception. This applies to you both, but most particularly to you, Queen Bethan. Do not take everything that occurs at face value."

"I will be on my guard."

"Good." She added in a softer voice, "Do not despair over Dalveen. You know of his resourcefulness and of his courage." She stretched her arm to indicate the army waiting below. They followed her gaze. "May good fortune attend you all."

Bethan and Quixwood turned back to her.

She had gone.

The only door to the tower, on the far side of the roof, remained firmly closed.

"I'll be damned," Quixwood muttered. "She's done it again!"

The pirates did not immediately attempt to board *Ocean Ranger*. But as grappling-hooks could be seen in the hands of the enemy crew, and boarding ladders were being positioned, that was obviously their intention.

"What are they hesitating for?" Shani wondered.

"I don't know," Leandor said. "But I doubt they're going to keep us waiting long to find out."

There was a bustle of activity on the pirate ship's deck. A group of a dozen or so men had appeared from below. They were lead by a tall, commanding looking individual in a plumed hat and silk finery.

"Their captain, I'll warrant," Leandor remarked.

"Looks a bit of a fop to me," Shani reckoned. "What's going on over there?"

Her question was answered by what happened next. The enemy captain drew a rapier and held it aloft. And the men he had brought with him raised their weapons.

"Archers!" she exclaimed.

"Take cover!" Leandor yelled. *"Bowmen!"*

The pirate captain's sword went down. His signal unleashed the first round of arrows.

Two places along from Leandor and Shani a man spiralled to the deck, a wooden shaft in his chest. A scream came from the rigging above and another fell. In all, six or seven Delgarvians were felled.

"*Keep down, everybody!*" Leandor shouted.

The archers sent over another barrage.

An arrow buried itself in the rail a pace from Shani's head. Several other men took hits and collapsed into their comrades' arms.

The pirate ship was moving closer. Boarding ladders were being pushed over the side. Here and there men were swinging ropes with grappling hooks.

A further swarm of arrows arrived. They claimed just one Delgarvian this time. Everyone else had flattened themselves.

"We're sitting targets!" Shani complained.

"They're hoping to keep us pinned down until they can get their men aboard. Then the archers will have to stop for fear of hitting their own people."

"That doesn't do us any good *now*, does it?"

"It can't go on much longer. They're about to—"

There was a tremendous crash as the pirate ship side-slammed into *Ocean Ranger*. The impact sent shrieking men plunging from the rigging.

Grappling-irons flew across and bit into the rail. Boarding ladders and planks snaked nearer. Pirates were readying themselves to swing over on ropes.

More arrows cut the air.

Leandor drew his sword and leapt to his feet.

CHAPTER 22

A boarding plank slammed down on the rail in front of Leandor. Instantly a pirate began rushing over it, cutlass in hand.

Leandor drew back his sword, waited a second for the man to get into range, then slashed at him. The blade sliced across the pirate's legs. He shrieked and toppled off.

Two more men were already on the board and running towards him. He plunged his sword into the deck and took hold of the plank, straining to dislodge it. With just one arm against such a weight it proved impossible to budge.

Suddenly his sergeant was beside him. "Let me help, sir!" he yelled.

The running men were more than half-way across. Leandor and the sergeant heaved mightily and managed to lift their end of the board. They flipped it on edge, sending the screaming pirates to the water below. The board crashed down after them.

Leandor snatched up his sword. The sergeant turned to meet other raiders swarming over the rail further up. Shani was exchanging cutlass blows with a man twice her size.

Along the whole starboard side, Delgarvian troopers were hacking at the pirates trying to get on board. In one or two places, defences had been breached entirely and the enemy were flooding over.

Shani felled her opponent with a thrust to his guts. He was replaced by another. She double swiped his face and left him twitching on the deck.

An arrow shot past her ear and embedded itself in a mast. Others downed two or three Delgarvians. "Hell's teeth!" she cursed, and shouted to Leandor, "I thought you said that was going to stop!"

"Try your knives!"

"What?"

"Your *knives*! Try them!" He turned away to duel with a new arrival.

"Why didn't *I* think of that?" Shani muttered.

She looked down at Tycho, sheltering in a corner. "Hold this for me!" she yelled, tossing him her cutlass.

He caught it and replied, "I'll watch your back for you!"

She plucked a knife and gazed over at the pirate ship. The bowmen were still in the same place, taking careful aim at individual *Ocean Ranger* defenders. She got a bead on the archer standing nearest to his rail.

Her blade spun through the air and struck him in the face. It was unlikely to have been fatal, but it put him out of action. She grabbed another knife and judged the force necessary to hit her next target. He was further back and the throw needed to be harder. The effort paid off with a hit square to his chest.

"Shani, look out!"

She spun to heed Tycho's warning. But at that moment there didn't appear to be anyone directly threatening her.

The homunculus pitched the sword back to her, at the same time shouting, "*Above!*"

A pirate was swinging at her on the end of a length of rope. He dropped to the deck and immediately attacked with his cutlass.

Hand-to-hand fights were raging all over the deck. Some were one on one, others were brawls between groups. Screaming and shouting rang out on all sides. Men slipped and skidded on pools of blood.

Leandor finished the pirate challenging him with a clean stroke to his heart. Then another flight of arrows winged over and he had to duck fast. Nearby, one of his troopers took a shaft in the neck.

That decided it. The archers were doing too much damage. Leandor was going to carry on Shani's work and try eliminating them. He glanced across at the enemy ship and saw the captain barking orders. If he could be killed too, that would be even better.

A pirate jumped on board, a cutlass in his teeth. Lunging forward, Leandor ran him through, his sword tip stopping only when it met the wooden rail the man had fallen against.

Tugging free his blade, he looked for the sergeant. He was near enough to be called over. "I'm taking the fight to them," he told him. "Want to come?"

"Yes, *sir*!"

"Can you find two others to go with us?"

"No problem." He hailed a pair of troopers who had just dealt with their opponents. They ran to obey.

"I'm going for those archers, and if possible the captain," Leandor explained. "But this isn't an order. I want volunteers."

"We understand," the sergeant replied.

The troopers nodded eagerly.

"Then let's go. And good luck!"

He led them to the nearest boarding plank, cutting down any who got in his way. A couple of arrows swished in their direction but passed harmlessly.

Leandor was first on the plank. Before he reached the middle, a man stepped on to the other side and charged at him. They crossed swords and the pirate caught a blow in the midriff. He staggered and plummeted over.

The enemy ship now had less men on its deck than *Ocean Ranger*. But Leandor's tiny group still met fierce opposition. They battled their way through a forest of blades, leaving a trail of dead in their wake. The archers were still firing. And the captain, who like them had not noticed the approaching foursome in the chaos, continued bellowing orders.

Shani pulled her cutlass from a dying man's chest and swung it at a second brigand. Its edge caved in the man's skull and he dropped like a stone.

Tycho clutched her sleeve. "There are too many! We must withdraw from here!"

"Where to, for the gods' sake?"

"There seem to be less at the stern! It might be possible to hold them off there!"

She cut down a pirate dashing past and yelled, "All right! Follow me!"

Their way was littered with corpses and discarded weapons. Numerous fights continued, with the enemy still swarming aboard. Shani was in no mood for gentle persuasion. If she couldn't go around a living obstacle she carved her way through.

Tycho was the object of more than one blow. Blades, knives and clubs bounced harmlessly off his supernaturally toughened hide, leaving his attackers stupefied.

As they passed a Delgarvian trooper a grappling-hook flew over and buried itself in his back. The line it was attached to pulled taut and he smashed into the rail. Shani quickly severed the rope. But her comrade was beyond help.

"The odds are too great, Tycho," she said. "We're losing!"

"Keep going!" he urged.

On the deck of the pirate ship, one of the troopers with Leandor went down. The sergeant lashed out and killed the man responsible.

They were close to the pirate captain and his archers now. Looking up, the captain saw them. He shouted something to the nearest archer. Leandor's second trooper ran ahead and was felled by an arrow.

The captain backed off, putting more men

between himself and the remaining pair of charging Delgarvians.

Then Leandor crashed into the line of archers and laid about them with savage fury. Several dropped their bows and drew swords. Two or three fled. One swiftly notched an arrow, meaning to unleash it point blank. Leandor's blade cleaved through bow, arrow, string and flesh. The sergeant stood shoulder to shoulder with him, claiming his share of lives.

Most of the bowmen were dead or mortally wounded when the sergeant was lost, going down under a hail of blows.

Shani and Tycho reached the raised stern section. She got to the stairs first. A pirate was galloping down.

Charging up the steps, she head-butted the man in the stomach, knocking the wind out of him. He doubled. She grasped his legs, heaved him up like a sack and tossed him over her back. He crashed down the stairs behind her, Tycho moving nimbly to avoid being hit by him.

When they reached the top of the raised section, actually the roof of an after-cabin, they found no one else there. At least, no one alive. They looked over to the pirate ship and saw Leandor in the thick of the fighting. He laid a man out as they watched.

A thundering on the stairs dragged them away

from the sight. The pirate Shani had just thrown down had climbed back up. And he wasn't happy. She didn't wait to hear his complaint. Her boot connected with his chin and he tumbled down again.

"I'm so sorry I was made in such a way that I cannot help fight these ruffians," Tycho apologized. "I feel so useless! I—*Shani, look!*" He pointed to the deck below.

A brazier had been overturned. Its red-hot coals scattered everywhere, several into a small lake of lantern oil. Flames were sweeping across the deck. They rapidly reached a mast, and the blaze ignited a dangling sail.

Shani saw that only a few Delgarvians were still on their feet, and that another fire had broken out at the ship's prow. Men were already throwing themselves over the side, one with his clothes aflame.

The nearest fire had spread to the stairs they had just climbed and was consuming them. Sparks and ash floated up. They backed into the rail at the stern.

"We can't go back down there," Tycho said. "We have no choice but to go over the side."

Shani turned and stared down into the sea. It was a long drop. "Must we? I was never too fond of heights. Or water, come to that."

"In that case, Shani, forgive me."

He pushed her overboard.

Then dived after her.

Shani wasn't anywhere to be seen. Tycho splashed around frantically, looking for her.

Suddenly her head and shoulders broke the surface. She spat out a mouthful of water. "I thought you weren't allowed to harm humans!"

"I wasn't harming you, I was *saving* you. Come on, we have to get away from the ship or risk being sucked down with it."

They swam to a piece of floating wreckage. It was barely big enough for both of them to hold on to.

"You cling to this," Tycho said. "As I never tire I have no need of it."

Totally ablaze, *Ocean Ranger* was slowly sinking nose-first. They could hear distant screams.

They caught a brief glimpse of Leandor. He seemed to be the only Delgarvian on board the pirate ship, and he was surrounded by a large group of men. The enemy captain stood before him with a rapier in his hand.

Then Tycho and Shani's makeshift raft was swept away by the current.

Leandor was aware of his ship slipping beneath the waves behind him but he didn't take his eyes off the pirate captain. He had no idea what had happened to Shani and Tycho, or whether any of his men had survived.

All he wanted to do at that moment was sink his blade into the grinning pirate chief's heart.

Eyeing the heavily-armed men all around him, he calculated whether he could reach his target before they got him. He took a step forward.

The captain and all the men quickly moved back. A long way. Considering the odds were at least thirty to one it seemed overly cautious. He took another step.

Leandor glimpsed a shadow on the deck, and heard a faint sound above. He looked up.

Too late. A large fishing net, hemmed with lead weights, had been dropped by men in the rigging. It fell straight towards him.

And covered him, striking with such force he was knocked flat. His sword was dashed away.

The pirates roared with laughter. He tried to get up but the heavy net prevented him. Stretching his fingers, he strained to reach the sword.

Then the captain came over and stamped his boot down on Leandor's hand.

CHAPTER 23

Torpoint felt empty without Dalveen, Tycho and now Golcar. Yet when night fell, Bethan's only wish was to be alone. She dismissed her ladies-in-waiting and retired to her chambers.

In melancholy mood, she sat for a while at the dressing-table, combing her long blonde locks in front of a mirror. At length she put down the brush, then glanced again at her reflection.

Avoch-Dar stood behind her.

Bethan screamed. She spun around, a hand to her mouth. The sorcerer leered unpleasantly.

Before she could speak, he said, "Summon the guards, by all means. But they will not hear you."

She knew he was telling the truth. There was no

doubt his magical powers could stifle the sound of her cries for help. Determined to act in queenly fashion, she defiantly returned his penetrating gaze.

"What do you want of me, vermin?" she demanded.

He greeted her fortitude with a short, cold laugh. "Merely to console you on your loss."

"You have already mocked my father's death."

"I did not mean your father. I refer to Nightshade."

"Liar! He lives."

"Loss can take many forms, my dear. Death is one way. A man's decision to make a new life for himself is another. Either could result in you never seeing him again."

"What do you mean?"

"Why, Leandor's … *affection* for Shani Vanya, of course. Come now, don't tell me you are not aware of their feelings for each other?"

"They are friends, comrades at arms; no more."

"If you say so."

"To imply otherwise is a wretched slander!"

"Perhaps. But has it never occurred to you that Leandor would have much more in common with another warrior than a nobly born lady like yourself? They would feel an affinity, you must see that. It is only natural that they might be tempted to share a common destiny."

"Your foul inventions cut no ice here."

"You will see it differently as time passes and Leandor does not return. But let us hope for your sake that death is what keeps him away. That would be better than constantly wondering what he and she—"

"Enough! I have been warned to beware deceptions, wizard."

"And very good advice it is, too. But think, my dear, of who may be deceiving whom."

She had no answer. Despite her resolve, she was shaking.

"It is so sad," he continued with fake sincerity, "that you should be deprived of a king to sit at your right hand and help you rule. Of course, *my* services are still—"

"You fiend!" she shrieked, snatching up a silver powder box.

She threw it at him with all her might. The box passed through the sorcerer, bouncing harmlessly across the rug beyond.

Avoch-Dar's laughing image faded, then vanished.

Tears were running down Bethan's cheeks.

She knew that the wizard was a master of lies. But she could not rid herself of the thought that there may have been truth in his words.

Drew Hadzor thought it might be pleasant to die.

It was the only release he could hope for from Avoch-Dar's cruel captivity. The monk had seen too much, heard too much, it was more terrible than his worst nightmares.

Now death would be a blessing.

Bound to the marble column in Pandemonium's Great Hall, powerless to determine his own fate in any way, the events unfolding about him seemed like a dream. Or yet another nightmare in the making.

Avoch-Dar and Berith made no attempt to hide any of their dealings from him. It was as though they regarded him as less than the lowest form of animal. The Sygazon seemed to think of all human life that way. With the possible exception of the sorcerer.

Depleted in body and spirit, burning with fever, Hadzor was dimly aware that the depraved wizard and the hellish creature were conversing nearby.

"There is no doubt," the demon lord rasped, "that an outside force interfered with your conjuration of the storm. The tempest should have pounded the ship to oblivion, yet something prevented it reaching its full, ungovernable power."

"Do you know who or what stayed it?"

"We have our suspicions, and in due course you shall know of them."

"But at least the Delgarvians were snuffed out. And Leandor is as good as dead, considering the hands he has fallen into."

"Whether that is so or not, the time has come to move

to the next stage of our plan. *The book is vital to this. As we proceed, its hunger will grow many-fold, and the gifts it will bestow in return will be wondrous indeed. It must be fed, Avoch-Dar, and fed constantly."*

Hadzor turned his weary, fearful eyes to the Book of Shadows.

And thought that if death were not available, perhaps the oblivion of madness would give him release.

Shani and Tycho drifted for hours, and now it was dark.

The icy cold water did not trouble the homunculus, but Shani's limbs were so numb she could no longer feel them.

Now they were being taken towards a large strip of land, which they decided must be the island of Nordelph. When finally they could see the shore, Tycho added his strength to the current and their piece of wreckage was washed up on the beach.

Shani was exhausted. She crawled ashore, and once clear of the waterline could do no more than stretch out on her back in the sand, gasping for breath. Tycho left her there as long as he dared.

Eventually he asked, "Are you feeling any better?"

"A little."

"Well enough to walk? Because this is a very exposed place, and we really should try to find shelter."

She agreed, and with his aid made it into the tangle of undergrowth and trees at the top of the beach. They hid themselves there for several hours more, until some feeling returned to her battered body.

Sitting with her back to a trunk, her strength restored a little, she said, "What do you think happened to Dalveen?"

"I do not know. But let us not forget that his fighting skills are unsurpassed."

"I believe you're just saying that to make me feel better. Even a fighter as good as him would have found those odds overwhelming."

"We have no proof that he is dead. And if we are to help him, we must first help ourselves."

"The only thing is, we're not exactly in a marvellous situation, are we? This is a dictatorship, run by some tinpot tyrant, so we're not likely to find it that welcoming. On a purely practical level, you can't fight, and I'm not what you'd call in perfect condition at the moment. I don't have my cutlass, which I lost when we jumped, and I've just two knives left. And assuming we can even get *off* this island, we—"

"Yes, Shani, I am aware of the difficulties. We must take one step at a time. Our first move should be to find a village or township. Fortunately I do not need food or drink. But you do. When that is taken care of, we may be able to obtain a weapon for you. Then we can look for a ship to take us away from here."

"You make it sound so simple, Tycho. But what you say is true; even the longest journey begins with the first step. Let's get moving."

They headed inland, keeping the few roads they saw in sight, but staying off them. The terrain was mostly scrub and marsh, which made the going harder for Shani. Finally they came to a small settlement and concealed themselves in the trees while they surveyed its layout.

"Well, it's not much of a town," she decided, "but it should have what we need."

"Do you have coins with which to make purchases? Or will it be necessary to steal the items we require?"

"I've got a little money in my boot for emergencies. It's better to pay our way, stealing's too risky."

"Very well. But it would also be a risk if I were to accompany you. My appearance—"

"Yes, I'd thought of that. You'll just have to stay here, out of sight, and I'll get back as quickly as I can."

Shani dusted herself down, smoothed back her hair and slipped out of the trees.

There weren't too many people about, but those she saw looked cowed and grim. A result of Nordelph's harsh government, she assumed.

The place was barely a village, consisting of just a few houses, a couple of barns, a blacksmith's and a tavern. She couldn't see anywhere that seemed to be selling anything. Reluctant as she was to draw attention to herself, she decided to make enquiries at the inn.

She found there were only three customers, all men and each sitting on their own. The person serving was a plump, middle-aged woman.

"What can I get you?" she asked pleasantly enough.

Shani ordered a drink and seated herself at the counter. She took a sip of the wine and said, "I need to purchase some supplies. Can you tell me where I could find a merchant?"

"There are none here, my dear. Is it food you'll be wanting? Vegetables, meat and the like?"

"Yes, among other things."

"Then take the road leading west, ride for about twenty minutes and you'll come to a farm. They'll sell you produce."

Shani thought it best not to mention she didn't have a horse. She meant to put that right next, at the blacksmith's. "Thanks. And where's the nearest armourer?"

"Armourer?" The woman looked surprised. "You're new to these parts, are you?"

"Er, yes. Why?"

"That would explain you not knowing about

240

the law. Citizens are not allowed to own arms on Nordelph, on penalty of death."

"Now you come to mention it, I remember now. Silly of me." Shani quickly finished her drink. "Well, I'd really better be moving. Thanks again." She left smartly, afraid she may have aroused curiosity.

After she'd gone, the woman beckoned to one of the solitary drinkers. They had a whispered conversation. Then the man hurried to a back door.

Shani didn't think she had made a particularly good job of the encounter. So she decided it would be wise to obtain a pair of horses as quickly as possible and rejoin Tycho.

The blacksmith's main entrance was shut, not unexpectedly given the time of night, but a scribbled note directed her to a door at the side. She turned into the alley running beside the building.

Half-way down it, her instincts told her she was not alone. She turned. Four men were following her. There was enough moonlight to see they held swords, despite any law to the contrary. She hurried on, hoping to outpace them.

Four more men, also armed, appeared at the alley's other end.

She reached for one of her two remaining knives.

Then she noticed she was standing next to the blacksmith's side door. The two groups of men were getting closer. She pushed at the door. It opened.

Swiftly stepping inside, she found the place in darkness. Unable to see a thing, she took a cautious step or two.

Then someone grabbed hold of her from behind, forcing her arm up behind her back. She started to struggle. A length of keen, cold steel pressed against her throat. She froze.

The door she had come through opened. She was aware of a number of people entering, no doubt the men who were stalking her. Someone lit a lantern.

They faced her in a semicircle, hard-looking individuals with no nonsense expressions. The one she hadn't seen yet still had the dagger to her neck. A slightly older man, who may have been the group's leader, pointed to the knife in Shani's hand.

"Drop it," he said.

Shani hesitated. If they were going to kill her anyway, there was nothing to be lost in putting up a fight. Old habits had her wondering what chance she had of breaking the hold of the man behind her before he started cutting.

But she was too tired, and too dispirited.

"To hell with it," she muttered and tossed aside her knife.

One of the other men came forward and searched her. He found the only other blade she had and slipped it into a pocket. The man holding her let go. She rubbed her arm.

"Who are you?" she asked, noting they wore civilian clothes and were unlikely to be some kind of militia.

"That doesn't matter at the moment," replied the one she assumed was their leader. "But we want you to come with us."

"Do I have a choice?"

"Not really. So far you've been sensible. I hope you're going to stay that way, because we'll have to blindfold you."

She had to submit to that, and to having her hands bound behind her back.

"Don't make a sound," the leader added. "It's just a short walk to where we're going, and then I promise we'll untie you. All right?"

She nodded.

They bundled her out of the building.

The short walk turned out to be not as short as they promised. Or perhaps it seemed longer because she couldn't see where she was going. It also occurred to her that they might have been doubling back on their route to keep her confused.

Eventually they arrived at another door and she was pushed through. Then they walked her across what must have been a room, because their footfalls echoed on wood.

"Stop," the leader ordered.

Her blindfold was taken off. She faced another door. Somebody reached over and opened it. A flight of stone steps led down into darkness. Probably a cellar.

"I'm sorry," the leader told her, "but you're going to be our guest for a while." He cut through the rope binding her. She felt a gentle shove in the small of her back. Sighing, she started down the stairs. The door was slammed and locked behind her.

When she got to the bottom, she found the cellar wasn't totally unlit. A single candle burned on a rickety wooden table. Apart from that there was just a couple of chairs and a lot of straw scattered about the place. There was no window or any other way out apart from the door.

She hadn't a clue what was going on or who her captors might be. Nor could she imagine what they wanted with her.

At least she could console herself with the thought that they didn't get Tycho.

Over in a corner, a pile of straw moved. She tensed, ready to defend herself.

The straw moved again. Somebody, or something, was uncovering him, her or itself. She hefted one of the chairs for use as a makeshift weapon.

The figure was getting to its feet.

It moved towards her and stepped into the circle of light.

"Hello, Shani," said Tycho.

With a mixture of relief and disappointment, she dropped the chair. "So they got you too. I was hoping you'd managed to escape."

"I tried. But it came to the point where violence was called for, and of course I couldn't act."

The homunculus seemed strangely sombre, even given their circumstances.

"Are you all right?" she asked.

"Yes. I mean no. They could not harm me physically, as you know, but…"

Shani was puzzled. "Go on."

"The hurt I have is not in my body, yet the pain is great."

"You're not making sense." She was worried. "Where is this pain? What caused it?"

"I suppose it is in my mind. I am not sure. I have so little experience of those feelings you humans call emotions. As to its cause, it was brought on by words."

"Words?"

"Yes. I hurt because the men who brought me here told me something." He hesitated. "Something about a friend."

A terrible sense of foreboding gripped her heart. "What did they say?" she whispered.

"Shani … Dalveen is dead."

Look out for the spine-jangling new crime
series from Malcolm Rose:

LAWLESS: Brett. Detective Inspector
with a lot to prove. Biochemical background. Hot
on analysis but prone to wild theories. *Dangerous.*

TILLEY: Clare. Detective Sergeant
with her feet on the ground. Tough and
intuitive. Completely sane. *She needs to be.*

THE CASE: *1. The Secrets of the Dead*
Four bodies have been found in the Peak
District. They're rotting fast and vital evidence
needs to be taken from the corpses. You need
a strong stomach to work in Forensics...

THE CASE: *2. Deep Waters*
Colin Games has died after a bizarre illness.
A post-mortem reveals no obvious cause of death,
but the pathologist isn't happy. Enlarged liver,
anaemia, heart irregularities – it all points to *poison...*

Join **Lawless & Tilley** as they pick over
the clues. But be warned: it's no job
for the fainthearted.

Point Horror

Are you hooked on horror? Thrilled by fear? Then these are the books for you. A powerful series of horror fiction designed to keep you quaking in your shoes.

The Claw
Carmen Adams

The Bride
The Cemetery
D.E. Athkins

The Dead Game
Mother's Helper
A. Bates

The Surfer
Linda Cargill

The Cheerleader
The Return of the Vampire
The Vampire's Promise
Freeze Tag
Night School
The Perfume
The Stranger
Twins
Caroline B. Cooney

April Fools
Help Wanted
Fatal Secrets
The Lifeguard
The Mall
Teacher's Pet
Trick or Treat
Richie Tankersley Cusick

Camp Fear
My Secret Admirer
Silent Witness
The Body
The Stalker
The Window
Carol Ellis

Vampire's Love
1. Blood Curse
2. Blood Spell
Janice Harrell

Funhouse
Prom Date
The Accident
The Invitation
The Fever
The Train
Diane Hoh

Sweet Sixteen
Francesca Jeffries

Driver's Dead
The Yearbook
Peter Lerangis

The Watcher
Lael Littke

Hide and Seek
Jane McFann

Point Horror

The Forbidden Game:
1. The Hunter
2. The Chase
3. The Kill
L.J. Smith

Amnesia
Dream Date
Second Sight
The Boy Next Door
The Diary
The Waitress
Sinclair Smith

Spring Break
The Mummy
The Phantom
Barbara Steiner

Beach House
Beach Party
Call Waiting
Halloween Night
Halloween Night II
Hit and Run
The Baby-sitter
The Baby-sitter II
The Baby-sitter III
The Baby-sitter IV
The Boyfriend
The Dead Girlfriend
The Girlfriend
The Hitchhiker
The Snowman
The Witness
R.L. Stine

Thirteen Tales of Horror
Thirteen More Tales of Horror
Thirteen Again
Various